PROVIDENCE, OI

HI PHOENIX!!!

THANK YOU SO MUCH. HOPE YOU LIKE THESE STORIES. AURYNN HAS TOLD ME MUCH ABOUT YOUR TENACITY.

PROVIDENCE, ON ALL FOURS

SHAUN PHUAH

PROVIDENCE, ON ALL FOURS

Edited by Melchior Dudley

To my mom, thanks for everything.
Thank you also to the friends who are my family.

Copyright © 2021 Shaun Phuah

contents

Outside a Denny's in Chicago at 1:00 a.m.   1

Anger in the Late Night   7

Angry Raccoon   16

Maggie   20

Gracious Gift of Hunger   23

Au Naturel   62

Providence, on All Fours   66

Who Does What   88

Strange Weather Ahead   92

Hunger in the Heavy Heat   103

Diphenhydramine, for Allergies and Other Things   108

Nourishing Itself on the Walls of Our Home   113

Despicable Blue Pig   127

Deep Green Gravity   131

Outside a Denny's in Chicago at 1:00 a.m.

I hate these giant restroom mirrors because I always end up watching myself shit. Bare ass on the toilet seat, I feel walked-in-on and visually assaulted at the same time.

I flush, wash my hands, wipe them on my jeans, and walk back out.

The food's arrived at our booth, and Mafaaz, a small, black-haired woman, is holding a burger dripping with sauteed mushrooms.

She barely looks up at me as she eats, starving at the end of her shift.

"Everything come out okay?" she asks.

Sitting at my table is a small BLT sandwich. The bacon looks burnt.

"I don't like that you were just thinking about me taking a shit this whole time," I say, squeezing some ketchup out on my plate. "But, yes. Everything came out okay."

She laughs and puts a hand on mine.

Another late night at the Denny's. The pale yellow lights of the restaurant mix with my lack of sleep to induce a haze. I put the sandwich in my mouth and crunch against bitter burnt bacon edges. Mafaaz is halfway through her burger.

"How was class today?" I ask, through a mouthful of bread and bacon.

"Same as always," she says. "Half the class has dropped out now."

"Shit, seriously?"

"Yeah, but the nurses and the profs expect it. Most people sign up and can't deal with the stress."

"I bet."

She takes another bite of her mushroom burger and puts it down. "Mateo, I can't work at the restaurant anymore. It's too much. The customers just piss me off, and I'm done with the disrespect the cooks give us."

I nod. We've been working together at the same Mexican restaurant, and the food is as authentic as its cooks, who don't know how to make refried beans, and who have somehow managed to burn mushrooms to a black, unidentified carbon-based lifeform. The hours are brutal, so Mafaaz and I tend to end up in a Denny's with no other place to eat so late at night.

"I know," I say, "I found this coffee shop that's hiring. I put my résumé in yesterday, so fingers crossed."

She nods and finishes her burger. Mafaaz came over from Egypt when she was a kid, ended up in Chicago, and got stabbed a couple years later by a dude named Terry in freshman year of high school after he broke a milk bottle over a table and jabbed her with the sharp bits.

As a kid, she saw her dad die of poisoning while in Egypt and later got her ribs broken on a boat after a fall. Sometimes they'll hurt, but she says there's really not much you can do about broken ribs unless you get surgery, and that's just crazy expensive.

Once, a tiny rib bone poked out her side, and she said, "Oh shit, see! Touch it!"

I touched it and it was sharp. She put a bandage over it, and it never happened again. She thinks the ribs have more or less healed now.

"Yeah," she says, "I've sent my résumé to some other places, too. We just need to get the fuck out of this restaurant shit."

"Jones yelled at you for like a half-hour yesterday."

"I know! And soon as you say something back, he hates it, and then he hates you for months. It's shit."

"Only good thing about working there is when Blind Tino comes in," I say.

Mafaaz's face brightens and she smiles. "Oh my god! Yeah, he's always coming in with that golden retriever."

"Even better is when he comes in with that bottle of tequila."

Mafaaz laughs, "Oh yeah…the smoothest stuff. He must get it from Mexico or something."

"Yeah, I think he said he gets a bottle every time he goes back."

I finish my sandwich, and we sit in silence for a moment. She comes up close and rests her head on my shoulder. She's warm.

A few more moments of silence pass, and I wrap my arms around her and kiss the top of her head before saying, "Alright, come on, let's go home."

She nods, "I'm so ready for sleep."

We pay for dinner and walk out. I feel bad for the waitress—the bags under her eyes have bags.

We leave the restaurant and walk down the street. White light glows from the streetlamps above, and our breath can be seen in the night air, a sign of the brutal winter to come. Some of the trees still carry red leaves, but most of them are bald. With each step we take, a light crunching follows.

Someone's walking towards us. He's wearing a bright blue hoodie and is shivering.

A couple more years of school and Mafaaz will be a registered nurse. Maybe I should go back to school, maybe something vocational, be a mechanic or something. I pick things up pretty quick, and anything seems better than washing dishes and cutting vegetables for people who yell through half my shift. We'll save up money and move somewhere a little better. Somewhere less cold, I'm hoping, but somewhere better than the cramped apartment we're living in now. The west coast has al—

There is a screeching sound. A rumbling noise that gets louder and louder. The ground shakes, and I can hear wheels grinding on asphalt. Mafaaz squeezes my hand, gasps, and stops.

The man in front of us is bathed in bright yellow, and he looks up before a car slams into him, ripping his legs off and throwing his body a few feet in the air before he lands again in the distance.

Mafaaz lets go of my hand and runs to the man.

I can't move. I'm breathing so fast, and I can't stop.

His legs land in the middle of the street and bleed. The street lights turn the pavement blood black.

The car door opens, and a bony white woman stumbles out. The smell of alcohol is a sticky mist surrounding her.

"Oh shit, oh shit, oh shit," she says, running with no coordination to where Mafaaz is tearing off fabric from his mangled blue hoodie and tying it around his thighs, where it begins to soak.

The woman sees the body and screams.

"Oh my god!" she screams, over and over again.

"Mateo!" Mafaaz yells, but I don't hear her. I'm looking at the man, legless and unmoving, and I'm stuck and still breathing too quickly.

"Mateo!" she yells again. "Call the fucking police!"

This connects, and I pull my phone out of my pocket. My hands are shaking so hard I can barely type 9-1-1.

The drunk woman is sobbing as another car tries to drive through, and the woman waves her hands, all frantic, "Don't go! Ther—he's been hit!"

I tell the operator on the line where we are and what's happened, and I watch Mafaaz pressing down on his chest—one, two, three, four, one, two, three, four—and where his legs used to be is just a gush. The road is a glistening mess, and I can't see the blood where the lights aren't shining. The man is silent and unmoving, except for Mafaaz and the second-by-second pumping. She keeps going until red and blue lights flood the street.

Four in the morning now, and we're back home. We walk through the small living area and head to our bedroom, too tired to turn any lights on. We shower together without saying anything, and I watch as the water goes over the caked-up blood on Mafaaz's hands, and the shower floor blooms red like someone's put a paintbrush in a clear glass of water. I get some soap and wash blood off of her where she can't see it.

We get into bed and I hold her close.

"He was dead as soon as he hit the ground," Mafaaz says, "maybe even sooner."

"I can't get it out of my head," I say.

We're silent as the heating in the room kicks up and whirrs warm air through the vents. She pulls me closer until both our bodies are touching. I can hear her breathing in the dark.

"I'm gonna have to think about this whole nursing thing, Mateo."

"Yeah?"

"Yeah. I'm really gonna have to think about it."

"I get it," I say, "I love you."

"I love you too."

I don't manage to sleep, and I watch my curtains flowing in the dark until yellow-morning sunshine bleeds through the fabric, high beams cutting the night.

Anger in the Late Night

    Tommy's acting all odd, pacing back and forth, full of anxiety—I can feel it coming off him as he walks up and down the wood floorboards. Some moths have managed to survive into the early winter and are bouncing off the dim orange lights glowing around his little wood cabin.

    "She knows, doesn't she?" Tommy says, looking up from the ground for the first time to stare at me.

    "I don't know anything about your situation," I say. He's been acting strange ever since I came into the cabin. Fidgeting and looking at the ground, staring off in the distance, agitated, the smell of stress pungent in his sweat when he walks by. His eyes keep glancing over to a locked wood door by the fridge.

    "Christ, you wouldn't like it," Tommy says, "you'd be so disgusted. God, you'd hate me for telling you."

    It doesn't sound good. Last week's snow has thawed out into puddles of grey water outside the cabin window, and I look down the muddy pathway to the lake in the distance, black and still under pale clouds.

    I figure it's best to get his mind off this panic, so I say, "I got a tour of a slaughterhouse recently."

    "What." Tommy says, looking up at me. He walks over to where I'm sitting by the wood table, where a single dim floral lamp casts long shadows around the room, and he sits down across from me. His leg jackhammers up and down. "You mean you just went and did that for fun?"

    "No," I say, "it's a friend of mine down south. He just wanted to show me that animals can be killed humanely."

Tommy looks up at the window and then back to me. "Y'know, I don't think I could go to a slaughterhouse. Don't think I could handle that smell."

I nod. "It did not smell good, that's true. But he showed me how they do it."

"If I could go anywhere, it would be the ocean. In the middle, where I couldn't see anything else."

"It's mostly humane, I think. Him and his workers brought a cow up to show me— it was gonna die whether or not I was there— and they took one of those things…y'know…that bolt pistol thing? Bunch of compressed air pushes a metal thing into the cow's head, and it's pretty much over in a second."

Tommy shakes his head. "They line up though, no?"

"What, you mean the cows?"

"Yeah, I mean, they know what's coming, right?"

"I don't know. Never interviewed a cow before."

"They have to know, I mean, they can probably smell something's wrong. Blood and shit and piss everywhere? I mean, they'd have to know."

"It's hard to tell what an animal's thinking about," I say.

"I think that fear gets in our food, that adrenaline and panic— I bet their bodies start making all kinds of hormones."

"Maybe you're right, but I'm not some scientist."

"Cows only smell that way in slaughterhouses."

"Okay, no, I can see that, but all I'm saying is that at least when they go out, it's quick, y'know? That makes me feel better at least."

Snow starts coming down in big congealed snowflakes that begin to cover the ground outside. Tommy sees this through the window and it pushes his panic into full gear as he stands back up and rushes to look outside.

"Fuck! It's snowing, fuck, fuck, fuck!" Tommy yells.

"What's wrong, man? You're acting so strange."

He takes a breath and looks at me, then his eyes glance over the locked wood door. "I've done something horrible."

"You know you can talk to me, man," I say.

"I need you to know that I'm ashamed, I shouldn't have done it, but I did, and I'm ashamed, and you ought to know. I think you ought to know, I trust you, and you probably should know."

"I don't know what you're talking about," I say.

"I'll show you right now," he says, and walks over to the wood door. He puts his hand in his pocket, pulls out an old metal key, and unlocks the door.

He pushes the door open and I look into the room. Pale grey sunlight beams through the open windows, revealing an almost barren extra room. The walls are made of brick, the wood floorboards are full of dust, and in the far corner is the body of a little boy, curled up against the corner of the room. He has no shirt on, just a pair of pyjama pants with a fabric design of little peeled bananas all over.

I walk to the body of the young boy and see that he looks perfectly preserved, the way a vegetable in vinegar retains its full shape and structure.

"He's dead," Tommy says, "he was dead like this when I opened the door."

"He really is dead," I say, not daring to touch the body. I can see that a thin sheen of dust has settled over the backs of his palms and in the small dip of his ankle.

"I left him in here maybe...ten minutes, and I don't know what happened, I opened the door and he was dead there, and it looked like he had been dead there for a long time. Like I just opened the door and his body had been there since the start."

"This is your boy," I say, "isn't it? God, I'm so sorry."

There's a knock on the front door, and Tommy jumps in place. "Oh fuck! I think that's Linda."

Tommy runs out of the room and up to the front door. "I'll just be a second, honey! It— we're just trying to get a fire started. We'll let you in when it's done."

"What? It's coooooold out here!" Linda yells from outside.

"Imagine how much warmer you'll be when the fire really gets going," he says.

A moth larva, with a white body like condensed milk and a tiny, hard brown head, wriggles across a slit in the wood floor and meets me by the edge of my boot, and says, "I saw what happened last night, I did."

I bend down low to speak with it better. "What? You saw what happened?"

"I did indeed, I saw it all happen, late night and full of snow, and I saw it happen alright, with my own eyes, I saw it, I saw everything."

"What did you see?"

"It was nothing but big red anger in the late night. It's what I saw, was big red anger, bright enough to warm the whole cabin, better than any fire ever could. It was nothing but big passion, big, big passion. You should've been here to see it."

"Did Tommy kill his son?" I ask.

"We animals see all sorts of things. All sorts of things. We're watching when people think they're all alone, and I've never judged you people once. I've never judged any of you."

"You're just a worm," I say, "you don't even know what you're saying."

"I'm a worm now, but I've stored up enough energy to be a moth. Imagine everything I'll be seeing when I'm flying about. I love the corners of walls, because people—you people never pay attention to things that are out of sight, the most important things."

"Tommy would never hurt his child," I say.

The moth larva shakes its little head. "You people are so different in the morning and then so different at night. I can never know with people, so hard to tell who they are at what time of day. Tomorrow, I will be a moth, worthy of lamplight. Maybe you will still be a coward, maybe something more dangerous."

More knocking on the front door outside, and Linda's voice coming through: "I can't feel my fingers anymore, Tommy! What's taking so long?!"

"He's a liar," the worm says, "he doesn't know what he's doing. It's just instinct now."

"Fuck you, worm," I say, standing up, "he's my friend."

I walk out of the room and close the door behind me. I think about grabbing the worm's little body and smearing its creamy ceramic-coloured body between my fingers but decide against it. Disgusting animal. Months ago I had a moth infestation in my house, and always their larvae appear between the folds of containers, my fingers brushing against their soft bodies by accident and causing them to plop on the ground, wriggling in the fear of being discovered.

I look up at Tommy, and he's pale, mouth opening and closing like he's thinking about what to say, absent-mindedly tapping his fingers against his thigh.

He looks up at me now, "I'm so fucked, Koh, Christ.... I—"

There's more knocking on the front door, urgent now. "I am freezing!" Linda yells from outside. "Is Teddy sleeping? Koh's supposed to be here too, right?"

"Yeah! He's right here with me!" Tommy yells.

"Okay! Let me in then, I can see the fire coming through the chimney! I'm cold! Are you hearing me?"

Tommy looks at me and takes a deep breath. "You have to back me up here, he was like that when I found him."

I blink at Terry, and he doesn't wait for my reply, as he's gone up to the front door. He peers out the door's window for a second, unlatches the lock, and pulls the door open.

There's a suction sound and some bits of snow come in as Linda steps through, covered in fresh white snow.

"Hoooh!" she breathes, rubbing her fingers together and walking up to the fire. "Finally, god—you know when you get so cold you start getting warm again? Not a good feeling."

Tommy walks towards her and quietly says, "There's something you should know," but he says it so quietly that she doesn't hear.

"Where's Teddy then? Sleeping, I bet." She looks at me and smiles, removing her toque and brushing the snow off. It melts quickly into small puddles of water that seep between the cracks of wood on the floor. "He'll sleep all day if you let him."

"There's something you should know," Tommy says again, audible now.

Linda's slow to register the strange atmosphere as she unzips her flannel coat. "Sure…what's up?"

"Something… something happened to Teddy in the night. I—I don't know what happened, but something happened to Teddy."

Linda's staring at Tommy now, and it's total silence except for the fire licking away at wood and causing small pops.

"Where's Teddy?" she asks.

"I don't know what happened, Linda, it was—it was like I walked in there and he was just like that, I don't know Linda, maybe he got sick—I really don't know what happened, Linda."

"Where is he?!" she yells.

"In that room!" I say, pointing at the closed door.

"Koh!" Tommy yells at me, and his eyes are massive, and his hands and knees are shaking. He looks at Linda. "Yeah, he's there, but I don't think you should look. It's not right."

Linda runs over to the door and pushes it open so hard it slams against the brick wall, and I know she's seen the body because she's screaming, and she's run into the room, and now she's just calling her son's name over and over.

Tommy's breathing so fast. Panic pushes him forward and into the room, and not knowing what to do, I follow him.

Linda is crouched over the body of her child, her arms over his shoulders trying to wake up the still body refrigerated by winter weather.

"Teddy! Teddy! Oh god, Teddy!!" she's screaming, pushing on her son's arms, trying to stir him. I look at his feet now, and I see grey and brown moths, hundreds of them, appearing from between the slits of the floorboard, crawling onto Teddy's feet, moving up towards his thighs, congregating over his exposed skin.

"Linda, stop! Please!" Tommy says, running over to her and hugging her from behind.

She screams at his touch, turns around, and pushes Tommy away, causing him to fall over on his side, and she's breathing hard and staring at Tommy like some bull, and yells, "What did you do?! What did you do?! Whatdidyoudo!?"

"I didn't do anything, Linda!" Tommy yells back, and Linda shakes her head, eyes now red and streaming with tears, and she runs right past me, through the main room and out the front door.

"You fucking useless—Koh! Don't let her run away! She's panicking! She might hurt herself!"

But I just stand and watch as Tommy gets up off the floor and runs out the door after Linda.

I watch from the doorway as Tommy sprints up behind Linda, his feet kicking up big plumes of snow, and he grabs her from behind, wrapping his arms around her waist.

She screams and thrashes about, trying to free herself from his hold, when he lifts her high up off the ground and slams her back down into the snow.

There's a loud crack, and Linda's body goes stiff.

Tommy stares down at Linda's body, taking it in, snow falling in big sheets already starting to bury his wife, and he looks at me in the doorway. He points down close by where her head is, and says, "There was a rock here I didn't see. The snow covered it, I hadn't meant to—"

He breaks eye contact with me and looks ahead at the massive expanse of white snow ahead, blowing in, covering everything in a big soft layer, an ocean in the distance. He looks back at me for a second and runs off into the approaching snowstorm. White flakes quickly pile up on Linda's body, and where her head had hit the stone is a big bloom of bright red leaking onto the ice like thick cherry syrup on a snowcone, and soon enough her body is obscured by snow burying her in.

I turn around, run back into the cabin, and open the door to Teddy's dead body, and see that the moths have covered him up to his neck and many have started dying and hardening on the boy's body, creating a grey-and-brown cocoon.

The larva is still here, watching its elderly in their process, and it turns to me. "None of this will go to waste," it says. "We will turn him into something beautiful, something deserving of lamplight."

Angry Raccoon

    Feeling full after a big dinner and standing under the conical green glow of a city street-lamp when Junho passes me her pink vape pen and says, "Christ, you see that raccoon? That's one chubby bitch."
    I breathe deep on the pen, taste artificial raspberry turning my lips numb, and feel the nicotine like warm water dripping down my back and pooling in my chest. The raccoon has got a plastic wrap in its hands and is slowly munching away at potato chip crumbs. "It looks like the Hindenburg," I say.
    Junho laughs. "It looks so fuzzy...and round."
    "You think it'd let me pet it?"
    "Don't!" Junho yells, taking the pen from me.
    "It looks really friendly though."
    "Raccoons do weird things, man."
    "Okay, but this one looks like it's just having a good time hanging out here, y'know?"
    "So don't fuck with it."
    "Yeah, okay, but I mean it looks like it's having such a good time that it'll just relax and let me pet it y'know?"
    There's a rustling sound as the raccoon digs deeper into its chip bag, fingers greasy and full of red-orange potato dust. It digs its hand deep into the bag and searches with its fingers for a moment for more chips before it decides to plunge its whole head into the bag for more food.
    "Okay, that's very cute," Junho says.
    The raccoon's massive, almost perfectly spherical butt waddles awkwardly as it tries to get the bag off its head.
    "Alright," I say, "I'm gonna go up and pet it."

"Li-Yang, don't do it."

"Why not?" I say, already walking towards it.

"If this thing bites you I'm gonna have to drive you to the hospital for rabies."

"Yeah, but you're like the best driver I know," I say, now almost at touching distance from the raccoon.

I can hear the thing breathing in the bag, searching for every last morsel and licking the inside clean. Its fur is smooth, a perfect gradient of grey and black. I extend my fingers, move closer to the raccoon, shift my feet as slowly and quietly as I can, and I lean in a little closer and press my fingers up against its back.

The raccoon instantly stops moving, the plastic bag still on its head. It becomes completely quiet in an instant. I look up at Junho, and she's got her hands on her mouth and is staring at me and the raccoon.

I look back down at the animal, my fingers still touching its back, neither of us moving. I lift my hand up to pet the back of its neck when it rips the chip bag off its head and reaches into a hidden pocket at the very front of its body, impossible to see until it has its hand deep into the fur, and pulls out a handgun.

"STAY THE FUCK AWAY FROM ME," the raccoon says, "you think you can just come up and just…and just fucking touch me?!"

"Holy shit!" I yell, falling back and putting my hands up as I stare at the gun in my face.

"Li-Yang! Oh my god, it's got a gun!" Junho yells.

"What—what, you making fun of me? You making fun of how I look or something? You think I'm cute and chubby? Think that means you can just fucking come up and scratch the back of my head like I'm some house cat?"

The black paw holding onto the gun is shaking. The raccoon stares at me with its black shadowed eyes, puts a paw around the base of its neck, and pulls off its raccoon head to reveal a slightly smaller raccoon head that looks exactly the same underneath.

"What the fuck?! You're just a smaller raccoon hiding in a big raccoon?" I say.

"It's difficult living out here, okay? The bigger you look, the less likely it is that some angry dog is gonna come up outta nowhere and end your life right then and there. This suit is my life."

The raccoon is breathing heavy and we can all hear it in the silence as the thing keeps pointing the gun at me.

I hear "Oh my god, oh my god, oh my god…" coming from the bushes to the left of me when something pops out of the leaves. I see it's another raccoon walking up to us on its hind legs, and it reaches up to its head with its little black paws and pulls off its fuzzy raccoon head to also reveal a smaller identical head underneath.

"What are you doing, Clarence?!"

"I've had it with these fucking people, Morris, and I'm gonna shoot this guy right in his forehead."

"What the fuck?!" I yell, staring at the gun, the raccoon's finger on the trigger, its whole hand shaking.

"RELAX. Clarence, fucking relax," the other raccoon says. "I found some popsicle sticks, Clarence, big haul tonight. I tell you what, I got like ten popsicle sticks in my bag."

Clarence's big black eyes are getting wet and I can see its frustration with its teeth bared and its fur standing straight up. He takes a deep breath and says, "You got a bunch of popsicle sticks?"

"Yeah! I got so many and we can share 'em. I'll give you seven."

"You'll really do that for me, Morris?"

"It's no problem. You've obviously had a bad day."

And now I hear the sound of footsteps rushing up at us, thudding loud against concrete, when Junho appears behind Clarence—who's still got the gun in his paw—and in a single, fluid movement, she runs up beside the fuzzy raccoon, lifts a foot up, and punts the bastard up and away into the night air, where he lands in the bushes twenty feet away.

"CLARENCE!" Morris yells, and he runs off after his buddy.

Junho grabs my hand, picks me up, and we go running off into the night, hearing Morris searching for his friend in the bushes behind us.

Maggie

I am awake. It's late, and my room is dark except for moonlight, lines of pale grey coming through my closed curtains. There is a horse beside my bed. I can't move.

The horse is large and unmoving. Most of what I can see is its silhouette in the dark.

"Maggie," someone says. "Move closer. I wanna have a closer look."

The horse doesn't move, and my eyes follow the source of the sound.

"Maggie, you're too far. I can't get a good look."

I see the movement now. There is a man's face growing out of the horse's side. It is a smooth face, devoid of all hair. No eyebrows or eyelashes, his eyes big and staring out. He is just half a head jutting out close to the horse's thigh. There are folds of skin like a pug's head that ripple out from the face, a puddle of loose flesh.

"Maggie. Move closer to him." His voice is clear. He is not bothering to whisper so late at night.

I'm trying to move my body, but I'm stuck lying on my back with my arms to my sides.

The face moves slightly in the folds of skin and his eyes meet mine.

"You're awake?"

I'm trying to say something, but my mouth won't open.

"Maggie, he's awake," the face says, "I want to be there for him."

The horse doesn't move.

It stands so its head is facing the windows while its backside is by my head.

"Maggie, please, get in closer," the face says.

I am trying to move my body, but I am stuck—my body feels stitched to the bed.

The face starts squirming, like a caterpillar that's been sprayed with an insecticide, side to side, bending the folds of skin here and there.

"I'll do it, Maggie. I'll do it if you don't listen."

The horse doesn't react.

The face opens his mouth and stretches as far as he can to where it reaches the horse's thigh, and he bites down hard. He gnaws away, moving his half-a-head from side to side. The horse groans. It sounds like a person in discomfort, a low moaning like someone with a hurt stomach. It starts to move backwards, and the face begins to get closer to me.

There's a mumble that's growing in the back of my throat. Some sound that's starting to materialize, trying to push past my vocal cords, and the face is inching closer.

The face lets go of the horse's thigh, and it says, "That's good, Maggie, I'm getting closer."

The sound pushes past the folds of my throat, and I say, "You're making her uncomfortable!"

"What was that?" the face asks.

"You're scaring her. I don't think she likes that."

"Oh…no. You don't understand—she's used to this."

"What are you doing? Why are you here?" I ask.

"I wanted…I wanted to say goodnight. Give you a good smooch goodnight is all."

"That's okay," I say, "I don't need a kiss goodnight. I was sleeping fine already."

"Oh…" the face says, "but I oughta give you a smooch anyway. It makes it so nothing bad can happen to you in the night, only good dreams."

"I never remember my dreams anyway."

Maggie backs close enough to me to where I can feel the face's hot breath on my forehead now, and he says, "Okay Maggie, that's enough, you can stop now."

The horse begins to move a leg back, and the face stretches back to the thigh and bites down again to make the horse stop. I can see the indents of his teeth in the horse's flesh. I can see the old bite marks, too, some of them scarring over, a web of soft tissue.

The horse stops with this second bite, and the face is now right next to mine.

"I told you I don't need a goodnight kiss," I say.

"That's okay, I'm already here anyway," the face says.

He moves his lips forward, and they're warm and wet against my forehead, and he's giving me long kisses up and down my face, leaving a messy snail's trail of saliva as he does so.

"Goodnight," he says, kissing me up and down, "goodnight, hope you have sweet dreams. Goodnight, I love you, goodnight."

I can hear Maggie crying. Deep, long sobs, and I can see the horse's body vibrating with every heavy inhale.

Gracious Gift of Hunger

The setting sun is glowing in deep oranges, reds, and pinks in the distance, low enough now to be able to almost look at directly, though bringing my eyes to its centre feels wrong—sunlight overexposes in my iris and causes an itching sensation within the walls of my pupils.

The rays of orange, red, and pink melt into each other and spread across the sky like spilt paint, while solitary white clouds in the distance absorb the colour and float above us fluffy and slow, like massive chunks of cotton candy.

The sunset has spilt into the lake as well, giving everything an intense red and purple colour. It reflects itself against the birch trees in the distance, making everything look like it's submerged in a fiery mirage.

Close to the shore, some ducks swim about, their bright orange feet paddling slowly between clusters of lake foam.

"The water doesn't even look real right now," Samui says.

"Touch it," I laugh, "lick some."

"Pretty sure I saw a massive duck turd floating by just now," Laura says, picking up smooth, flat stones with her right hand and collecting them in her left.

"Ducks are friendly vegetarians anyway, right?" I ask. "Means they've got super clean poop. Just wait, someday duck poop will be a facial trend."

"You should start the trend," Samui says.

"They're friendly vegetarian rapists," Laura says, "I mean, look at them go."

Two green-headed male ducks follow a brown female duck around. They idly float around each other and pick at scraps in the water with their beaks.

"Hey, you leave that lady alone, you fucking perverts!" Samui yells, and the ducks collectively paddle away from the aggressive sound.

"Oh, they're just chilling with each other," I say, "maybe it's some kind of polyamorous thing."

"You know female ducks had to evolve corkscrew vaginas to deal with male duck assault?" Laura says.

"I don't know if you can call natural animal sex rape, Laura. Which one came first anyway, the corkscrew vagina or corkscrew dick?"

"All I know is that ducks are fuckin' delicious," Samui laughs.

"Bet a traumatised duck tastes way worse." Laura nods, leans back slightly, and flings a smooth stone sideways, and we all watch as it skids across the water five times before disappearing beneath smooth, orange water.

"All I'm saying is that you can't tell what animals are thinking, man. They just are, y'know? They're just there. No opinions."

Laura shakes her head. "They'll speak to you, you know? If you really know how to listen."

"You know…" Samui says, kicking coarse wet sand up, creating divots in the shore, and muddying the water, "as a kid I saw once, this momma crow sat up in a nest with a bunch of her little babies, and suddenly she's nudging the littlest one with her beak 'till it fell out of the nest and fell in some grass."

"Shit…" I say, "did you help the lil' baby out?"

Samui shakes his head. "Some fuckin' chipmunk showed up outta nowhere and ran off with it."

I feel a sharp pinch around my wrist and look down to see a thin black mosquito has landed almost exactly by the veins below my palm, and its abdomen is slowly growing larger, a bladder being filled, until I bring my other palm down on its body in a fleshy smack, leaving behind a black-grey smear and a blossom of bright red blood already caking up against the grooves of my skin.

Already the itch is there, and the swelling.

I push my thumbnail against the welt, press crescent indents across the bump in my skin, feel the itching subside slightly, and then euphoria in scratching.

The sun continues to set in the distance, and the brighter reds and oranges dim into deep embers that glow through the clouds in violet colours, saturating the water and draping everything in purple dusk.

The trees around us cast darker shadows now, longer, growing with each other: night's coming in, and with it a cold breeze.

"I'm glad we got to see this," Laura smiles, tossing a final stone into the water. She angled it badly, and it doesn't skip, just plunks into the water and sinks. "I always feel like I've caught something when I see a good sunset."

Samui nods. "Not every day you get to see a sunset like this."

"Yeah," Laura says, smiling. "I love sunsets. It feels like catching something special, like a rare butterfly with beautiful wings."

"Or a moth."

"A real gorgeous evening," I nod, and Samui slaps at something on his neck. Seeing this makes the bump on my skin itch;

it feels like the mosquito has injected millions of minute hairs underneath my skin, making me want to scratch at it, to break the skin and release all those insect hairs out where they belong.

I scratch at my wrist and feel a moment of relief before a duller itching comes back again.

Samui slaps at something on his neck and looks at his palm before reaching into his jean pocket and pulling out a teal pack of American Spirits cigarettes.

"Mosquitos hate the smoke, y'know?" he says, cupping his hands around the brown tip and lighting it on fire.

Tobacco smoke rises from the end of his cigarette, slowly filling the air. He blows smoke out through his nose, and it all stays static in the still atmosphere.

"Can I have one please?" Laura asks, walking up beside Samui, her hand already reaching for the pack.

"Oh, sure," he says, pulling one up for Laura to pluck.

"They're coming in with the night," I say, "we ought to head out soon…gonna be way more of these guys in a bit."

"Oh, relax," Laura says, taking a long drag and blowing the smoke around her. "These North American mosquitos are super stupid."

There is the buzz of something by my ear, and then a new itching sensation, a flare on the same arm but higher up, by my elbow, and I see the red skin and the white, bumpy middle, itchy itchy itchy. I reach over to scratch myself when I see it—in the periphery as I turn my head slightly, in the trees. Across the water where the land around the lake has made a crescent is the fleshy pink head of an animal, though it is just far enough away that all I can make out is the far-away blur of a face staring at us.

I stare back, and the itching in my wrist and by my elbow turns into a mild burning sensation. The face is by the birch trees in the distance, between the white trunks, its body hidden behind bark and foliage, the head unmoving. I think I can make out the eyes. I feel like I'm looking at someone.

"Do…you guys see that?"

"I've been trying to ignore it," Laura says.

"What the fuck? You've seen it this whole time?" I ask, feeling strange now. I look up, lose the face for a second, and can't see it in the natural patterns of the forest until my eyes pick up on its fleshy pink head again, and I see this thing in the distance, watching us.

"What are you guys talking about?" Samui asks, already halfway through his cigarette, the white ash collected on the tip like dead skin, sagging and ready to fall off.

"You see it there?" I ask. Putting my finger up, I try to point directly at the face in the far distance.

Samui squints his eyes. The sunlight is disappearing faster now, all the bright pinks and yellows gone and replaced by dark red and violet colours. He scans the horizon in the distance.

"Don't you see it?" I ask. "It's right there! In the middle of those trees, it's just…I don't even know what it is. It's just looking at us."

Samui bends his whole torso forward slightly like that'll help him, and I watch as the face between the trees disappears behind the foliage.

"Oh shit! I saw something move!" Samui yells. "Didn't really see it, though."

"Looked like…I don't know, looked like a face or something," I say.

Laura has been looking at the ground, eyes scanning the rocks though she doesn't pick any up.

"You alright, Laura?" I ask.

She looks up at me and I see the stress on her face. She's down to the end of her cigarette. She takes another puff, squats down by the rocks and squishes the yellow filter against a smooth stone.

"We should leave," she says, standing up, "something's wrong here. I don't know what it is, but that was really bad."

The itching in my wrist and by my elbows flares up—feels like there is something there beneath the bug bite, turning the risen skin numb.

"Freaky thing to say, Laura," Samui says, "you guys are telling me someone's watching us in the distance?"

"I—I'm not sure…I don't really…it was hard to see what it looked like."

"It was an animal," Laura says, "I could tell it was. But you're right. It was too far away to see properly."

"Alright," Samui says, shaking his head, "I'm fucking outta here. Let's go home. Nature was nice 'till it got fuckin' weird."

The tips of my fingers are getting cold, and I can feel it in my toes, too, cool air inhabiting the empty space in my shoes, and Laura nods, putting the crushed-up filter in her pocket.

Laura turns around, her eyes scanning the trees in the distance, and then the trees closer to us, their long shadows growing larger, filling up the air with solid black colour. The sunset is leaving us.

"Don't freak out just yet guys, come on," I say, fishing in my pocket for the car keys, turning around to head back to our parked car. The car is parked by the trees on the dirt road, with no streetlamps around. "We don't even really know what we saw. Just getting scared over some animal far away. Bet you it was a bobcat or something."

Laura's feet crunch against large lakeside rocks as she walks up beside me. "You saw it too, and you think it's a bobcat?"

"I don't know what I saw, but yeah. I mean, those things are everywhere. Sent my buddy's cat to the vet once. Those things are everywhere. Probably looking for food scraps or something."

"It had antlers," she says, "but a fleshy face."

Samui quickens his pace and walks faster than the rest of us, almost breaking out into a run to our blue car.

He waves his hands at me. "Come on, unlock it!"

I reach into my pocket, feel the rubbery buttons of my car key, click unlock, and nothing happens.

I press it again. The car's headlights do not brighten, and the car doesn't make a sound.

"Come on, man! Honestly, it's getting cold, too," Samui says, rocking back and forth on his feet.

I press down on the rubbery button with my thumbnail and still nothing happens. I press again and again, can feel the button beneath the rubber click, and I say, "I—I'm not…fuck. I don't know why. I think my key ran out of batteries."

I see Laura tense up beside me. Her head swivels around, scans the treeline for something.

Samui shakes his head. "Bullshit man, total bullshit. Totally trying to mess with me."

He reaches over to the handle of the door and pulls on it.

The door clicks and swings open, though none of the lights within the car turns on.

There is movement in the dark of the car, and a low hum.

Samui looks into the passenger-side seat for a second before he jumps back, wipes at his face, and starts spitting on the ground like something's flown into his face.

"Argh! What the fuck?!" he yells, "god, what…some bugs in my face or something."

I walk up to the driver-side door and open it up. Some mosquitos fly out of the open doorway, and I slap away at where I feel tiny legs landing.

"I got a light," Laura says, and she reaches into her pocket, pulls out her phone, and turns her flashlight on, casting a bright beam of white light into the driver's seat.

We now see what must be millions of mosquitos climbing over each other, a hive of them almost, their black and white bodies resting against the car seat to create a wall of insect wings, upholstery now made of sensitive insect hairs.

They have collected themselves on the steering wheel as well, so many of them that I cannot see past their bodies to the plastic and rubber beneath.

"What the fuck is this?!" I yell.

Samui is still spitting into the dirt and slapping away at his neck and face.

"That's disgusting," Laura says.

"Help me—help me get them out of here!" I say, leaning over into the driver's seat, and with my bare palms, I slap away at the steering wheel.

There are so many mosquito bodies that it feels like I'm pressing my palm against a larger, fuzzy body. When I lift my hand back up again, I see that it is a fleshy canvas now of mosquito bodies smeared against each other, pancaked by my palm, and I try to ignore the disgust and shiver going up my spine.

Laura's beside me, using the back of her hand to smack away at the mosquitos relaxing on the seat.

The mosquitos are frenzied now, and the sound of their high-pitched buzzing rises in volume and disappears again as their tiny bodies whiz past my ears, hover around my head, and attempt to land on my skin.

"Jesus Christ!" Laura says, dropping her phone on the seat and bringing her palms up to her face and backing away from the car. "They're biting the shit out of me!"

The phone on the seat shines the white cone of the flashlight straight up, and I can see now the mosquitos all around us, their bodies flying all around in the air, landing for a moment and then up again, and I look at the steering wheel, full of squished mosquito bodies and live mosquitos, layers of them on top of each other, and then I see that the steering wheel is full of insect bites.

The steering wheel's grey rubber has risen in multiple places. The spots where the skin has risen are white, while around the spots, red inflammation becomes more and more agitated.

I feel spots all over my body itching now, too, and with it comes an intense urge to scratch at the fleshy bumps on my steering wheel.

I can hear the sound of someone slapping away at their skin and Laura yelling, "Samui! Hey! You gotta stop! You're hurting yourself! Samui!"

With both hands, I continue slapping away at the mosquitos that are standing still on the solid surfaces of either the steering wheel or the seat or the armrests, my palms turning sticky with their ruptured bodies until I feel them against my neck, up on my face, needling their mouthparts into my skin, and I close my eyes so they can't be bitten and slap away at myself, scratch at what itches, and then there's more of them on my forearms, and I can feel them all over me now, crawling up beneath my clothes, and I yell out loud, thrash my arms about wildly, back away from the open car door, shake my body like a dog out of water, and slap away at what must be more bug legs landing on my body, though I cannot see them in the dark.

"Paul!" I hear the sound of Laura's voice behind me, but I don't dare open my eyes so long as I feel the sensation of bug legs brushing against the fine hairs on my body, and I keep flailing my arms up, hoping to scare the insects away, and slap away at the parts of my face that itch, my whole body turning hot and sweaty with inflammation.

"Paul! You need to stop freaking out!" Laura's voice again, and then something grabs at my arm, forcing me to open my eyes, and I see Laura beside me. She's got her hand wrapped around my forearm, and she's got her phone back in her other hand. All over her body, I see risen bumps turning red where the mosquitos have bit her, her neck red and full of scratch marks.

"We've got a serious fucking problem," she says, and I see that with my eyes closed, I'd panicked and moved far away from the car, which is now just a silhouette in the dark on the dirt road, a single door opened wide.

A mosquito and its high-pitched wings buzz by my right ear, and the bites by my ankles begin to itch.

"This is totally fucked up, Laura," I say, "the car's totally fucked, I don't even know how all these—"

"Something's seriously wrong with Samui," Laura says.

"What?"

"He's…I don't know, it's…it's like he's panicked too bad or something. It looks like a trance." She brings her flashlight up horizontally, and I see, not too far away, sitting on the ground and leaning against a tree, is the shape of Samui's body.

"A trance? What are you talking about?" I say, scratching at my ankles, feeling the soft risen skin with the pads of my fingers.

Laura walks over to where Samui is sitting and I follow her. She shines the flashlight against his body, covering him in harsh white light. He sits there with his mouth slightly open. His eyes are mostly closed, though his eyelids flutter up and down, revealing the white of his rolled-up eyes.

"Mehr…" Samui grunts, leaving his mouth agape as he tries to form words, "I've got it. I've definitely got it."

"Samui?" I call, though he doesn't respond to the sound of his name at all.

Laura puts a gentle hand on his shoulder and tries to rock him awake. "Samui, we gotta get going. We can't stay here."

The itchy red inflammation all over my body is making me sweat even though I'm shivering from the cold night air, and the sweat collecting in my armpits dries up to make me feel sticky and feverish under my clothes.

"Samui," I say, bending down to look at him better. He doesn't even notice either of us beside him. He mumbles something incoherent and moves his head to the right and lets it drop. "Samui! It's getting cold, man. We can't stay here, we gotta….we can't stay here all night."

"Shit…shit. This is really bad, Paul, something's seriously wrong with him."

"Samui! Dude! You gotta wake up!" I yell, grabbing both his shoulders with my hands and rocking him back and forth harder. His head flops backwards and forwards before I let him go, and his head thunks dully against the tree he's leaning against.

He raises his head, his eyes still rolled up behind his twitching eyelids, and he stands now.

"Samui? Fuck, are you okay?" Laura asks, and all Samui does in response is rotate his torso from side to side, letting his floppy arms swing about him until he loses his balance and falls back against the tree before landing flat on the ground, green grass and mud clinging to his face as he rubs it against the dirt, totally unaware.

All the sunlight has disappeared now, and all around us is nothing but dark night. Laura's phone flashlight is a single beam of white light shining through the forest, and she brings her phone up to her face, reads the screen for a second before she shakes her head. "The signal's fucked."

She looks down at Samui squirming in the dirt before she looks back up and points her flashlight down the dirt road, past my car, its doors still wide open.

"I think we gotta come back with help," Laura says.

I take a deep breath, can feel panic coming in with the dark. I'm scratching at the bites by my elbow, can feel the itch turning sticky, hot, and when I look down at my arm, full of risen skin, I see that I've broken some of the bites and that tiny blots of blood now polka-dot my arm.

"Okay…no, I think you're right. We gotta get out of here," I say.

Laura nods. "He'll be fine out here. We'll be back in an hour, max. All we gotta do is get some help back here. I…I don't know what's wrong with him."

"If this is a fucking stroke we gotta get help to him now!"

She nods her head. "You're right, but…never seen a stroke like this before."

She shines the flashlight on the dirt road again before she nods and says, "We gotta leave this way, I think."

"Okay, you're right," I nod, and with Laura's cone of white light fixed on the dirt road, she waves at Samui's silhouette and says, "We'll be back, Samui. It's gonna be okay, alright?"

We walk down the road with only this circle of light to anchor us. I feel something small fly by my ear, and I bring my hand up to swat at something that has either flown far away by now or is still circling around my head, waiting for the right moment to land.

Laura is quiet as we walk, our feet rushing through the cold night air and stumbling occasionally against uneven ground. I catch sight of her face occasionally when she accidentally clicks on the screen of her phone, and against the pale digital glow, I can see that she has sucked her lips into her mouth to bite on.

"God," I say, "I hope we can get Samui to a doctor in time."

"I don't think it's a stroke," Laura says.

"What? It looks like something's seriously fucked up his head."

Laura nods. "No, I think you're right, but...I felt it just then when I was tossing the stones...and that face in the trees. Soon as I saw that face it felt like the air got more humid or something."

I see in my head that face again, pink and far-away, between the trees, two dark eyes looking out at us from across the water. The crescent land anchoring us to each other.

Cold wind blows against us and I can feel my toes going numb and my stomach tightening up around itself. I shove my hands deep into my pockets to try to stay warm.

Looking over at Laura, I see she's shivering too, her whole body vibrating in the cold night air. Her eyes stay stuck to the ground, barely blinking, just putting one foot in front of the next. I see her hand gripping her phone and our source of light, holding on so tight the skin on her fingers has turned white in places.

There's a sound coming from our right: some sort of movement brushing against branches and a light popping in my ears like there's been the smallest change in atmospheric pressure.

Laura stands completely still and lifts her head up, watches the darkness like an animal—startled and on alert.

I stand here in the silence for a few seconds with Laura, don't hear any new sounds, and I say, "Just some random sounds, Laura, come on. Don't let it freak you out."

She stands still for a few more seconds before she looks at the trail ahead of us again and shakes her head. "Something's following us," she says.

I'm breathing faster now, and my feet move quicker without me thinking. "Why would you say something like that?!"

"I'm serious," Laura says, and I can see her eyes are large and panicked under the dim white light of her phone flashlight.

I'm trying to slow my breathing, trying to take longer breaths and shorter exhales, but my heart is pumping fast and I can feel it vibrating against the rest of my body, telling my legs to run.

"We're gonna hit one of the main roads soon," I say, "probably get a way better signal on your phone there."

Laura is quiet, doesn't say anything. She taps twice on her phone screen and it lights up. On her background is the image of a dead dog on fresh black asphalt against bright morning sun. The dog is a golden retriever, and I only know it's dead because she told me so when she showed me the picture some time ago. In the picture, it looks like it's sleeping. Its golden fur is slightly wet and dirty around the edges, but the dog looks peaceful. It has a red collar on, with a circular piece of metal with a single word inscribed: "Carlos".

Laura found the dog that way, on the street. Apparently, there was a huge patch of dried blood somewhere, though I can't see any of it in the picture. She thinks the dog was run over by a car. Got launched somewhere by the force of the impact and died. She loves the picture because she thinks dead things are still very much alive, that nothing has been wasted so long as she has this picture to look at.

In the end it's just another dead dog, though.

On the top right corner of her phone, I see we still have no signal.

There is the gentle sound of water somewhere ahead, some light coming in. At first, I think it's the dim fluorescence of a streetlamp, until we take a few more steps and I see that it's radiant moonlight peeking through the trees.

I'm watching my feet, trying not to trip over any more patches of hard earth, when I see Laura bringing the flashlight up in my periphery. She stops and gasps.

I look up off the ground and see that we have only walked back to the lake, the rocks here still disturbed from Laura picking at them earlier in the evening.

The lake is almost motionless, except for ripples near its edges from when cold wind comes through and settles in my clothes. The lake has absorbed all the black night sky and reflects it back at us. A single, nearly full moon sits massive in the night sky. I've only ever seen the moon like this a few times, closer to earth than usual, its gravity pulling my eyes to its centre.

In the middle of the lake is its equally large reflection, undisturbed in the water.

A mosquito hums by my left ear, causing me to slap at myself, and still, I can feel the sensation of tiny legs all over the back of my neck and by my ankles.

Laura screams, swivels her head around—looking at the treetops, back to the lake. She shakes her head over and over again and starts sobbing. "What's happening?! What's happening?!"

I can't stop myself from breathing fast, and it makes me want to scream, but I'm focusing on Laura and her panic so I don't freak out, so I run over to her and put my hands on her shoulders.

"Laura! You need to relax! W—we just got turned around, probably a turning we didn't see 'cause of the dark, y'know?!"

I feel something land on my neck and I let go of one of Laura's shoulders to slap at the mosquito. Laura shakes off my other hand.

"How long have we been walking for?!" she asks, slapping at the back of her ankles. "I kept thinking…I kept thinking, like, we should've seen some cars by now. Or, I don't know, the highway or something. It took us fucking five minutes to walk in here, Paul!"

It felt like we were walking for at least fifteen minutes. It could've also been a half-hour. I remember looking at the time on her phone, but the numbers aren't in my head anymore.

There's the sound of something stepping through dried leaves, a feeling of something in our space, and I whip my head around to look for where the sound came from.

Laura's done the same thing, her eyes darting back and forth from tree to tree. She lifts her phone up and turns the flashlight off. Moonlight shines down on us enough to see everything through pale silver light.

"Taaaaa-DAAAA!" It's the voice of what must be a small child, and then movement jumps out of a clearing in the trees just a couple of metres from us.

"Did I get'cha?" an excited voice rings out from the figure on four legs. It starts to trot towards us, and as my eyes adjust, I see that it is a medium-sized pig with antlers.

It trots up right up to our knees, and I'm so shocked I don't know what to say. I look over to Laura and it looks like she's calmed down enough to stop sobbing, though I can see her hands are still shaking.

I can see the pig properly now that it's right in front of us.

What I thought were antlers are actually gourmet mushrooms growing out of its head beside its floppy pink ears—many different species, all fruiting from the top of the pig's scalp: large trumpet-like grey oyster mushrooms, coral-like morels bloom in circles around the oyster mushrooms along with bright yellow chanterelles, and all of them jiggle and bob as the pig excitedly moves its head. I see that the pig also has shelf mushrooms growing out of its neck, creating somewhat of a halo, and on its neck are green and violet-coloured turkey-tail mushrooms and bright orange, red, and white reishi mushrooms, making the pig look a bit like a mushroomy sunflower.

Looking at its body, I see that its fur is fuzzy and white-pink as if peach fuzz has been allowed to grow unhindered all over the pig's body.

"Hehehe," the pig giggles, and trots up close up to me and rubs its snout against my shin, "scared you pretty good, I think, I really did, didn't I?"

"You're that face we saw!" I say, watching as the pig runs around in a small circle, wiggling its head from side to side, causing all the mushrooms on top to jiggle.

"I was! I was! And you guys were all so cool, especially you!" The pig laughs and walks up to Laura, does circles around her so that its fuzzy body brushes against her legs. "Your rock-throwing makes me wish I had hands!"

"We thought you were something dangerous," Laura says, letting the pig run close circles around her.

"Me?" The pig laughs again. "I'm here to save you from danger! This lake is dangerous, you know? Really shouldn't be out here. I saw you three from across the lake over there, and I knew straight away, gotta go help these guys out 'cause that lake's not gonna treat 'em well, and look! You're already trapped. All it took was two seconds, too."

"What? What are you talking about?" I ask.

The pig turns around and looks over at the lake water, full of night sky, the waters still even as the wind picks up and blows cold air through my clothes.

"This lake has turned bitter, didn't you know that?" the pig says. "And it cultivates mosquitos cos the waters don't move, didn't you know that? Such a bitter, bitter lake. Don't even know when it happened. It was like everything was fine one day, and then I turned around the next day and the lake was bitter. Bad water, and mosquitos everywheeeereee. So annoying."

"How do we get out of here?" Laura asks, squatting to talk to the pig better.

"Can't tell you! Caaaan't tell you!" The pig laughs and jumps up and down. "If I said it all aloud the lake'll hear and then it'll be all useless. Use your head or something, god."

"We—we've got a friend," I say. "Something happened to him. It's like he's in a trance."

"Oh…" the pig nods, "the third person. He does not need to go to waste."

"You're good, right? You're a good pig?" Laura asks.

"I'm soooo good," the pig smiles at us, "I'm here to save you all!"

"What's your name? You got a name?"

"Nope! Call me anything! No name, no name. All you gotta do is look at me!"

"Peach Fuzz," I say, "'cos of all that peach fuzz you got all over your body."

"Oh," Peach Fuzz laughs and nods, "well, you know, actually, I think that's mould! Showed up on me one day and started keeping me warm. Looks great too! Just y'know…don't breathe it in."

The silver glow of the moon shines above and below from the lake, and I can't help but stare and stare and stare, and I can feel something flying by the hairs on my arms and the small hairs on the back of my neck, and somehow none of it matters, and a great sense of calm moves through my body, and I know it is the same black-and-white static you see on an empty channel on TV.

"You're going to have to help me first," Peach Fuzz says, and I blink my eyes, realise I am still standing on solid ground, and look down at the small pig, its big eyes staring back up at me. It shakes its butt slightly and then says, "I mean…not me exactly, but my friend!"

"Your friend?" Laura asks, looking at the still waters ahead. "Why's your friend need help?"

"I don't know! I don't know!" Peach Fuzz shakes its head from side to side. "But you have to. You really gotta. All I know is my friend walked into the lake one day and never came back out."

"What are we supposed to do?" I ask.

"Swim! Float? Same thing, I guess," Peach Fuzz laughs, "but that's what you gotta do!"

I look over to Laura, and I see that she is still anxious and cold: her arms crossed and held tight against her, occasionally slapping at something at her ankles and scratching.

"Only one of you needs to do it." Peach Fuzz smiles and nods its head at me. "It should probably be this guy right here 'cause he's unathletic."

"That's very rude," Laura says, "he's only a little out of shape."

The pig gasps, "Why would you say that?! You want him to be bad at swimming! Don't you wanna get out of here?"

I frown. "I gotta swim in the lake?" I wiggle my toes in my shoes, can no longer feel the tips even as I press the ends of my toes hard against the soft fabric of my sneakers. "It's a cold night, Peach Fuzz."

Peach Fuzz rolls its eyes. "The water's not that cold, just bitter! Just bitter, bitter, bitter. Like when I go hunting truffles and eat earth! Bitter, bitter."

I look over to Laura, who's still got her arms held tight around her body, feeling cold, and she looks down at Peach Fuzz and says, "Our friend Samui…I'm really worried. Something might be wrong with him."

Peach Fuzz nods its head slowly. "Don't worry! Please, worry is bad. Your friend will not be wasted."

"I'm gonna do this," I say, "and then we can all go home."

I walk up to the lakeshore, feel hard rocks beneath my shoes melt into fine sand until I reach the meeting point of smooth, wet sediment and black, still water.

Laura walks up beside me and leans forward. Her eyes move up and I can tell her gaze has settled on the silver moon in the water. She looks up at me and says, "I think I saw something move in the water."

There's the sound of cloven feet stamping on wet sand coming up behind me.

"What like a fish or some—"

All the air is pushed out of my chest as two hard feet slam into my back, sending me face-forward into the water.

Cold water seeps into my clothes and presses against my skin, turning everything numb. A feeling of panic shoots up my back, asking me to breathe, but I ignore the urge and then open my eyes and see nothing but empty, black space.

The cold ebbs away, and in a moment I suddenly feel very warm.

I turn my body around and cannot see anything. I push my arms forward and feel nothing but the slight resistance of water, and I know I am very far from shore.

Now TV static begins to fill my body, pixels of black and white, silver light, all pushing against each other filling me up from my toes all the way up to the top of my head, and I have forgotten how to breathe, though I never knew how to do it in the first place.

I float here for minutes or hours. I wonder if the pads of my fingers and toes have gotten wrinkly, and when I press my thumb and index finger together, I feel nothing but the warmth of a missing channel and its static.

I don't remember what I'm doing here, or why, though there must be some reason.

I remember now: Laura, Samui and I, sitting in my living room, about to play video games, and Laura switched to a wrong channel and saw nothing but the wriggling mass of white and black and grey. Samui had said something about how we shouldn't change the channel too quick. Oughta appreciate what the start of the world looks like.

That's what the start of the world looks like? Laura laughed then, looks like shit she said.

Samui laughed and said yeah.

                                         Something swims
                           by my ear.

              Some fish with a long body.

Maybe it was an eel,
                    and it swims down into deeper,
                                                darker
                                                      water.

I squint my eyes down at the bottom, where I last saw it disappear, and I see that deeper down is a soft, pink glow, pulsing bright and then dark over and over again, and against the pink glow is a shape, the silhouette of something massive.

I angle my body downwards and start paddling through the water towards the soft source of pink light shining from what looks to be miles from where I am.

Swimming has never been easier as I float effortlessly through black water, and though I'm not breathing, my lungs are content.

I continue to swim downwards, the water pushing against my body, when I see in my head now many mosquito larvae, their comma-shaped bodies moving around with jerky movements before finding still water to stick straw-like mouthparts out through the surface tension to breathe air.

A betta fish with a bright green tail swims up to a massive group of mosquito larvae and sucks them up into its mouth as the baby mosquitos scatter and disperse.

And I see now, Samui's laughing face, showing nothing but big white teeth, and I remember Samui had told me that back home in the Philippines, he'd caught someone once sticking plastic cups in the holes of monsoon drains. The guy had looked scared when Samui showed up apparently, knew he was doing something wrong, and when Samui asked him what he was doing, the man ran off as fast as he could. Samui then crouched down by the plastic cups and saw they were all almost empty except for a shallow pool of dirty water at the bottom. Samui walked around until he found a huge line of red solo cups stuck into the crevices of a big monsoon drain, all of them filled with varying degrees of water. Samui inspected each one until he found one that was full of long, white mosquito eggs, bunched up together, held above the surface tension of the water.

Samui brought all the cups with eggs home and knocked over the rest.

He fed his pet turtles with the mosquito eggs and then the mosquito larvae that hatched by the next day.

Days later and his turtle had gone missing, was no longer in its enclosure, and Samui had to pour the mosquitos out onto the pavement, letting them bake and shrivel under the Southeast sun.

I continue floating downwards, and below me, I see the silhouette become more defined as the pink glow beneath it becomes brighter, and I see that it must be some massive animal with four legs at the very bottom of this lake. I can feel the water around my body tightening around my chest and my head as the pressure builds the deeper I swim.

I angle my body downwards so I sink faster, and the pink glow now rises to meet me, and I can see bits of movement becoming more obvious all throughout the massive four-legged shape at the bottom of the lake.

I sink and sink and sink and sink and sink and feel the water get warmer and thicker the closer I get to the pink glow, and the speed of my descent starts to slow.

The animal below is huge. It must be the size at least of a humpback whale or some large ship, and staring at its legs, I realise they end in hooves.

More of the eel-like, long fish swim by me, and I see now that moving across the entire body of this animal are thousands of these fish.

I sink further, and the pink glow now cuts through the dark water to reveal exactly what the animal is, and I see that it is a massive brown horse with white spots all over its body, and I've sunk low enough now to see that suctioned to multiple spots all over its flesh are lampreys, gorging themselves on the horse's bountiful surface area.

The horse's eyes are massive and intensely bloodshot, and its mouth opens and closes as if it is gasping for air, and I can see the thick, ropey muscles and veins along its neck popping and straining with the effort. It moves its legs up and down in weak motions that only cause minor disturbances among the lampreys suctioned to its body.

I can tell that this horse has been here for a long time.

The water turns more and more viscous and dense the lower I sink until I am suspended here above the massive body of this horse.

A memory now enters my head, and it is all I can see.

Laura and I are driving along the highway, just the two of us listening to music, when a stag appears along the right side of a huge empty field. It's winter, and though there isn't any snow outside, the earth has been frozen into a singular, hard surface. Separating the field from the highway is a dried-up ditch.

The stag is running at full speed, its legs pushing it forward, matching the speed of our car.

Careful, I say to Laura, don't want this thing jumping in front of us, and I see her eyeing the stag as she keeps her eyes focused on the road.

The stag suddenly shifts to the left and starts running towards the highway, and the car lurches as Laura slams her foot against the brakes.

The stag leaps forward, though it has miscalculated the distance the ditch has put between the empty field and the highway, and its front legs angle forward in the air before its whole head crunches against the ditch wall and its body flops to the bottom with all the residual momentum of its jump.

Christ!!! I yell, and already, Laura is parking along the side of the road to check on the animal.

I am watching this horse struggling to breathe here at the bottom of the lake. I can see its chest creating a vacuum, trying to pull air in, its eyes bulge outward each time it tries, though I don't feel any disturbance in the water. At this distance, I can see that the horse's body must be as large as at least a few football fields.

I can see that all across the horse's flesh are circular bleeding wounds, some of them fresh and leaking blood into the lakewater, others scabbed over or puckered up and tender, trying to heal.

All across its body, the lampreys swim across each other, looking for flat skin to suction on to.

The horse moves its legs up and down again, and this causes the lampreys to scatter like flies before swimming back and settling down again.

The horse's eyes swirl around, looking at everything in a confused panic, and occasionally I can feel its gaze settle on me, though I can't tell if it recognises what it looks at.

More of the lampreys have begun to notice my presence in the water and investigate by swimming around me.

Their long bodies glide through the water in long S shapes, curving in and out. One of them now approaches me, and I see its jawless mouth, a perfect circle holding many sharp, dark yellow teeth within, its dopey eyes staring at nothing in particular while it swims around me, its flat head moving side-to-side, searching for something to latch onto.

The lamprey swims close to me now, near enough that I could reach out and grab it if I wanted to, and I watch as it moves close and butts its head against my clothes.

The horse below us opens its mouth and attempts another deep gasp of air, and I see its chest almost cave into itself with the effort—and in a moment, I know everything this lamprey is thinking.

I know that it does not see very well, just different shades of light and vague shapes that appear before it. It can feel vibrations through the water, can tell when something has shifted from miles away, can even tell when sand has shifted along the shore. I know that it feels so light gliding through the water. Various smells appear, mainly the smells of fruit and iron, and especially now, with me in front of it, a feeling of hunger.

Another lamprey has started to investigate me, and the first one swims up to my neck and starts to rub its smooth skin against mine.

The horse below me raises its head slightly in a panicked attempt to pull air into its lungs, but all it achieves is disrupting the sediment on the lake floor.

I feel horrible for this horse. I thought at first that maybe I could do something, get the lampreys off somehow, but the sheer size of the horse's body makes this impossible.

I feel a pinching sensation on my shoulder, and I realise that one of the lampreys has managed to bury its head beneath my shirt and suction itself against my skin and dig its teeth in.

I watch more lampreys swimming towards me from the horse, and I realise there's nothing I can do here, so I start to swim upwards. The water around the horse is so thick, and looking up, all I can see is the pink glow extending upward into black water.

I push my arms through the water and can feel myself moving upwards.

There's another pinch somewhere along my calf, and I am sure another lamprey has attached itself.

As I continue swimming upwards, I can feel the water turning softer, and I know that I am leaving the miniature gravity the massive horse created.

The pink light is behind me now, and I am again among black water, and I continue swimming upwards through the dark until I see silver light shining in through the surface tension above, and when I finally break through into the night air, I take in a deep breath and stare up at the massive moon above me, almost full.

I can feel smooth bodies against my ankle and back, and I know these are the lampreys that have attached themselves to me, and the waters are now freezing, forcing my mouth into a jittery shiver.

I look around me, realise I am in the very middle of the lake, and through the thin moonlight, I can see the alcove that the pig had pushed me from, where a figure standing by the shore must be Laura, with Peach Fuzz sitting down beside her. I raise my hand and wave at her, and she waves back at me.

I start paddling towards the shore, with my hands in front of me the way a dog swims, because the thought of extending my arms and letting the cold water flow in freely through my clothes and against my skin is too much.

I can feel a pinching sensation against my shoulder and around my calf, and I know that those circular lamprey mouths are sucked tight against my skin, grinding their sharp teeth against me to drink.

I keep swimming until I feel sand scrape my knees and I know I can stand.

I stand up in the waters, still high enough to cover up to my waist, and I start wading towards Laura, who is standing in front of me; I can see from here that she's been crying, can see the long, glistening streaks of tears that she wipes away with the bottoms of her palms.

I finally reach dry sand and am pulling my legs out of the water when Laura runs up and hugs me, her dry clothes absorbing the water dripping off me and turning patches of her yellow t-shirt darker.

Peach Fuzz laughs and runs around us in tight circles, the mushrooms that grow from its scalp bobbing back and forth with its little head movements.

She pulls away from me, and I can see that she is still crying: her eyes are red, and her eyelashes carry thick drops of water.

"It's over now," she says, "Peach Fuzz talked to me…explained things to me. It's all gonna be okay, Paul."

"What do you mean?" I say, stepping back and blinking, remembering the horse at the bottom of the lake struggling to breathe. "I did it right? Didn't I? I—I found these…" and then I feel a pinch on my shoulder, and I turn to look and see the smooth body of the lamprey, its head suctioned firmly to the back of my shoulder, and Laura walks over, grabs the lamprey by its tail, and yanks it off.

There is a popping sound, and a circle of tiny holes bleeding lightly on my shoulder.

"There's one more on my leg," I say.

Laura bends down, grabs its head with her hand, and pulls it off. I see the lampreys on the ground, squirming now that they're on land, scraping their bodies against hard, sharp rocks, their gills opening and closing, trying to breathe.

"Look, Peach Fuzz! It's those lampreys you were talking about," Laura says, squatting down and pointing at the wriggling bodies, confused on dry land.

"Mmmmmm!!! My favourite! My favourite!" Peach Fuzz laughs, walking over. It sniffs at the lampreys for a moment before it opens its mouth and starts biting into their bodies, slurping them up quickly.

A cold wind blows through, now mixing with the water in my wet clothes and forcing me into a shiver, and I can't stop my teeth from chattering.

"I—I—I'm freezing," I say, "I need….need new clothes."

"It's okay! It's okay, you did so well," Peach Fuzz says, swallowing the last of the lampreys. "The sun will be up again soon, and it will be a gorgeous sunrise. Soooo beautiful. Gorgeous sunrise like you've never seen before. Something special. Gonna warm you right up."

"Where's Samui?" I ask, looking up at Laura. She looks like she's in a daze, isn't really here, and she doesn't say anything at first.

"Where's Samui?!" I ask again. "That was supposed to do something, right? Where's Samui?"

Peach Fuzz nods and laughs. "I know where he is! I know where he is! Come on, follow me!"

With that, Peach Fuzz trots off in the direction of our car, towards the line of trees. I've got my arms held tight around my body, so cold I can't stop my muscles from tensing up, and I'm about to follow right behind Peach Fuzz when Laura grabs my arm, forcing me to turn around and face her.

"It's not what you expected," she says.

"What?"

"Peach Fuzz talked to me while you were gone, explained everything."

"I don't trust that pig, Laura."

"The lampreys. They're sacred creatures, you know that?"

"I...I don't know if I follow. There was some kind of massive horse at the bottom of the lake and—"

"And the lampreys know this! They're ancient fish. The first fish to understand the value of blood."

Laura's eyes are so wide, and though tears run down her cheeks, she doesn't sob, just wipes them away with the bottoms of her palms. She puts a hand on my shoulder and squeezes.

"It's over for Samui," she says, "I'm sorry, Paul. He's just not there anymore."

"What?!" I yell, looking past Laura to the treeline, where it's nothing but dark where the moonlight fails to reach.

"And Peach Fuzz, she's gonna help. Samui shouldn't be trapped like this, Paul. It's wrong."

"I don't know what you're talking about," I say, and walk past her and towards the forest, where I know Samui is sitting against the large trunk of a tree, our car only a few metres from his body.

Laura follows after me. "You have to trust Peach Fuzz."

I don't say anything and bend down to pick up a large, perfectly smooth skipping rock, just in case, and keep walking towards the forest with Laura following beside me.

It gets much darker the moment we walk past the treeline, and Laura pulls her phone up and turns the white flashlight on.

Cold wind blows against my wet clothes, and I can't stop shivering.

We keep walking until I see the shape of our car in the distance, along with a rustling sound a little further ahead. We move forward until we see the shape of Peach Fuzz's body, and there is the light smell of sulfur in the air like a sweaty sock, along with the pungent scent of garlic.

We take a few more steps towards Peach Fuzz when we see that the pig is standing over some large silhouette.

Laura lifts the light of her phone up, and I gasp and feel tears welling up in my eyes when I see that it is Samui, engorged in a massive growth of large, abrasive, black scales.

"Samui!" I yell, and run towards my friend.

Peach Fuzz is beside him, sniffing with its snout at the growth that surrounds my friend, covering his entire body up to his face. His arms and legs have all been covered under a thick layer of black scales, and he looks almost like a Russian nesting doll. The scales have attached Samui to the tree he had been leaning against when we left him to fend for himself.

The black scales smell strong of pungent garlic and sulfur.

I can see that Samui is still breathing as his nostrils flare up with each breath, though his eyes are closed in peaceful sleep. And now I see them—mosquitos flying up towards his face. Three or four of them at a time, landing against his cheeks and the exposed top of his forehead, and there they sit and drink for a moment, their bodies becoming large and engorged. And then, as they are fat and full, they stiffen against Samui's skin, turn hard, and the body of the mosquito turns into a new black scale covering the surface of Samui's face.

I turn to Peach Fuzz. "What are they doing to him?!"

"He is turning into something grand," Peach Fuzz says.

"I told you, Paul," Laura says, walking up beside me and putting a hand on where Samui's shoulder would be underneath the rubbery dark scales that cover him, "Samui doesn't deserve to be trapped like this."

"Let's get him out of here, then!" I yell, reaching over to where his arm must be. I dig my fingers into the scales and feel that it is a soft, breakable material. The smell of sulfur and garlic escapes as I break into the scales surrounding Samui's body, and when I have my fingers around a thick chunk, I pull it clean off.

I realise now that I am holding a massive hunk of black truffle in my hand, with its lighter brown interior staring back at me. Looking at Samui, I realise that the huge chunk of torn-off truffle has not revealed any of his trapped body beneath, though it should have.

"That's all he is now," Peach Fuzz says, sniffing around the open wound I created, thick with the pungent smell of feet and onion, "a truffle. Beautiful and complex."

More mosquitos land on Samui's face to feed, harden, and change.

Peach Fuzz walks closer to Samui to sniff his large truffle body, and I can't help but gasp when it opens its maw with its blocky teeth and begins to take large chunks out of Samui, revealing nothing but light brown truffle flesh beneath.

This disgusting feast forces a heavy flow of tears up to my eyes, spilling down my cheeks, and I watch Samui and his calm face, still breathing as he is being eaten, his eyes closed, mouth shut in a calm sleep.

I stare at this pig gulping down mouthful after mouthful of black truffle. I reach for the stone in my pocket, walk up close to the pig from behind, and I'm tensing the muscles in my arm up, ready to bring the hard edge of the rock down on the pig's head, when Laura grabs my arm.

"What the fuck are you doing?!" she yells.

Peach Fuzz does not notice either of us and has become entirely consumed by its feeding.

I don't say anything and try to wrestle my arm free from Laura's grip, though she has a firm hold on me.

"Stop! Paul! She's special! Paul!" Laura yells, using both her hands now to hold my arm down.

"Don't you see what's happening?!" I yell, yanking my arm back to try and throw the stone against Peach Fuzz's head when Laura grabs my hand and pulls it back down again before I have the chance.

"You don't even know what you're doing!"

"This animal is eating our friend, Laura! Fucking help me get it off him," I say, trying to stare her down in the dark.

She grips tighter until I can feel her nails digging into my skin, and I can already see those crescent-shaped marks that will be left behind.

"What is wrong with you, Laura?!" I yell now, and I can still hear Peach Fuzz gorging itself on the truffle flesh of my friend. "What the fuck are you doing?"

"It's not so simple, Paul," Laura says, and I can see her crying fresh tears now, "listen to me! It's not so simple as this."

I've managed to switch the rock over to my left hand, and I see Laura's eyes go big as she realises too late. I lift my arm up in a wide arc and throw it in the direction of the feasting pig with as much force as I can use.

The smooth stone obliterates a fragile yellow chanterelle blooming from the pig's scalp, and the rock continues its trajectory straight against the back of Peach Fuzz's skull. There's a dull, bony thunk, and the stone falls back to the ground.

QUEEEEEEEEEEEEEEEEEEE.
QUEEEEEEEEEEEEEEEEEEE.

Peach Fuzz is thrown forward with force and falls flat next to Samui. Its mouth is open wide in its horrible, high-pitched squeal as it trashes its legs up and down in pain, throwing up dust with its hooves.

QUEEEEEEEEEEEEEEEEE.
QUEEEEEEEEEEEEEEEEE.

Laura's eyes are wide open in panic, and she's yelling and running towards Peach Fuzz. "You stupid fucking—what did you do?!"

QUEEEEEEEEEEEEEEEE.
QUEEEEEEEEEEEEEEEE.

Laura's bends down towards Peach Fuzz. "It's okay! Peach Fuzz, hey, hey, it's okay! It's okay!"

Peach Fuzz only continues squealing and kicking its legs up and down in confusion.

"Peach Fuzz, hey! It's all gonna be alright, honey," Laura says, bringing her hand out and petting the pig's side.

The moment Peach Fuzz feels her touch, fear propels each of its limbs into frantic kicking.

QUEEEEEEEEEEEEEEE.
QUEEEEEEEEEEEEEEE.

Peach Fuzz then manages to finally right itself, and in a moment, has run off into the woods at full speed.

From the sound of twigs breaking in the distance, it is clear that the pig has gone very far.

The two of us stand in silence, listening as the sound of rustling leaves and breaking branches gets farther and farther away.

I bend down now to check on Samui. Peach Fuzz has managed to eat through a large portion of his truffle body, leaving a huge pit of exposed white and brown flesh. Samui's eyes are still closed in calm rest, though as I watch his nose, I can tell he is no longer breathing.

Laura's shaking her head now, "I—I need to take a walk or something."

"We should bury his body, Laura," I say.

Anger shows itself in her furrowed brow. "With what, our bare hands?"

"We can…we can find something," I say, feeling like I've done something horribly wrong.

"I'm taking a fucking walk," Laura says, walking down the dirt path towards the direction of the highway.

I stay here for a moment, next to Samui's body, thinking about what I can do to bury him. The low hum of mosquitos begins again, and I can hear one or two of them flying by my ears, and I can't help but slap at myself at the slight chance a mosquito could have landed.

I see Samui here, with most of his body converted to black truffle, now nothing but the top part of his face, and I see more and more mosquitos landing on my bare skin, flying away only for a moment when I shake my arms and legs only to land again somewhere else I can't see.

This begins a feeling of panic as I imagine the mosquitos doing to me what they did to Samui, so I get up off the ground and run after Laura.

I spot her easily through the circular light of her phone, and she doesn't react when I run up beside her.

We walk in silence for a while.

I try to say something to Laura, but I can't stop thinking about that horse at the bottom of the lake. And then Peach Fuzz eating those lampreys that I brought back to shore with me.

I can see now more of the details of the trees that surround us, and I realise that early morning sunlight is coming back up again.

"Maybe we can float his body down the lake," Laura says, "not like there's that much left of him anyway."

We should have hit the highway by now, or at least have heard the sounds of cars speeding by, their engines roaring past at a hundred kilometres an hour, enough power to shake the earth beneath my feet, but instead, it is just the sound of birds waking up in the morning, making their calls. One call causes two more to ring back, causing three more to ring back, causing others to respond, and others more to sing. Soon the whole forest is awake. Ambient sunlight reveals more and more of the tall birch, oak, and pine trees around us.

"I'm exhausted," I say, "how long have we been awake for?"

"No idea," Laura says, but she's smiling now as bright yellow and orange sunshine begins to glow past the treeline, "but I do love a good sunrise."

She turns the light of her phone off, and as we continue walking through the woods, sunshine the colour of egg yolk shines against our skin and begins to warm us up.

We continue walking, and it is clear to me now that we are back yet again on a familiar path. A few more steps forward, and I can see the edge of the lake in the distance, now brimming with sunlight, almost too bright to look at directly, hot enough to cause an itching sensation within the walls of my pupils when I stare for too long.

I look over to Laura, and she is not surprised that we've ended up back here again, either.

We walk over to where we know Samui's body is.

He is only a few feet away from where the car is, its doors still wide open from the night before.

The only parts of him that are still human are the top of his forehead, the ridge of his nose, his calm, closed eyes, and the tiny dip of his mouth, just above the top lip. Most of his truffle body was eaten by Peach Fuzz so that he looks like the top part of some half-eaten vegetable.

"Come on, then," I say, "I think you had the right idea."

Laura nods her head and takes a deep breath, and together, we lift him up. Laura takes the top of his head, and I take the eaten-up section of his truffle torso, and together we carry him towards the lake.

He isn't very heavy.

We reach the edge of the lake and put his body down against the water, where he floats, buoyant on the shoreline.

"We can do this Viking style," Laura nods, staring down at Samui's body bobbing up and down above gentle waves.

"You got a flaming arrow?" I ask.

"Shit…"

"That's okay, we'd definitely miss."

"So I guess we just push him out to the middle of the lake?"

"I think that makes sense to me."

We bend down low and push on his body hard enough that it starts to float out towards the middle of the lake, and we watch as his face catches warm sunlight, and again, I can't help but see him sleeping, even though I know that isn't the case.

His body continues to float slowly out to the middle of the lake, and Laura and I sit down on the smooth shore to watch his journey.

Talking now feels wrong somehow, and the silence is as comfortable as relaxing in a hammock on a warm sunny day.

Two ducks begin to swim by, a brown duck and a bright green-headed duck, dunking their heads all the way underwater and lifting their butts up to look for bits of aquatic plants.

The ducks cause ripples in the water as they feed, and the tiny, circular waves they make cause Samui to slowly drift towards the crescent-shaped side of the lake opposite of us.

"Awh shit…" Laura breathes, "we're gonna have to push him from the other side."

We watch as Samui continues to float slowly to the other side, where thick, brown-headed cattails sway in the breeze.

Samui finally stops when his body is brought to shore by lake waves, stuck along the line of lake foam.

The two of us start to stand up, ready to head over to the other side to push him out to the middle of the lake again, when we see in the distance a pink, fleshy face pop out past the treeline.

I can see the busted-up chanterelle clearly now that I know what it is. And together, we watch as Peach Fuzz grabs onto the top of where Samui's head is supposed to be with its teeth before running back into the woods with his body.

I look over to Laura and see that she is smiling, and she takes a long, deep breath and lets it all out again as a sigh.

Au Naturel

breaking through anger
in the early morning
to see bright yellow

                                          another day locked
                                    in dark grey rooms full of
                                    rainwater and dead fish

dead squirrel body
bloated by the neighbourhood,
preserved by early frost

                                          mouldy ginger root
                                      deflated and full of white
                                      fuzz. Soft when squished

bright white datura
flower swaying slowly its
thorny apple pricks my finger

                                        green pixels floating
                                   in the air when I turn my
                                     head after five grams

late winter night
someone crosses the street and
comes back and crosses

                                        blow-fly, iridescent
                                   in the afternoon sun
                                   cleaning its front legs

white mushroom in the
grass, threatening to destroy
my kidneys and liver

                              pink pills of Benadryl
                           cradled together in a
                           white cup and shaky hand

the datura pod
dries and then splits open to
reveal its brown seeds

                                 a cigarette tossed
                              into pristine blue ocean
                                        and floats

soaking dirty clothes
watching the water turn
grey and milky

                              dead squirrel body
                         deflating into loose hair
                              no one has bothered

trash island in the Klang
River when a monitor lizard
appears above all

Providence, On All Fours

INT. COUPLE'S TREEHOUSE - DAY

Bright yellow sunlight coming in through the windows. JIN (30) hears some animal like a donkey with a sand-paper throat braying in the distance before the sounds of birds singing takes up the empty space. He sees his wife is not in bed with him this morning.

Jin shuffles out of bed slowly. He opens a drawer next to his bed and puts on his glasses. A black flashlight rolls out and back as he opens and closes the drawer.

Jin walks to a larger nearby drawer and puts clothes on. A simple green T-shirt, jeans, and a coat. Their treehouse is gorgeous in the morning; it's lived-in with nice, colourful embroideries around the house. There are a number of half-finished embroideries in the drawer.

One of the embroideries, in its circular holder and sewn with blue and pink fabrics, shows the image of a woman bending down on all fours to pick up flowers.

Jin climbs down the ladder.

EXT. GARDEN IN THE WOODS - SAME

When he reaches the bottom, his feet crunch into bright autumn leaves, and he turns around to see MICHIKO (32), a woman with long, straight black hair facing him, standing by their garden and pulling out ripe turnips, rupturing the earth and spraying green leaves with brown dirt.

                MICHIKO
    He's watching us again.

Jin looks up, and sees in the distance and behind the cover of trees a naked white man, standing in the sunlight, watching them.

Jin stares him down, and the two of them make eye contact.

They stare at each other for many long seconds, and like an animal in the woods, the naked man disappears behind the treeline.

                MICHIKO
    Sixth day. I've been counting.

She pulls up another turnip.

                    MICHIKO (CONT'D)
               Getting closer, too.
               I've been watching
               it.

                    JIN
               What do you think he wants?

                    MICHIKO
               Fuck if I know.

                    JIN
               He's just trying to freak us out.

                    MICHIKO
               Well, it's working.

Mid-autumn and all the trees are bright red and orange. Jin bends over and starts helping Michiko with some of the turnips, roots like fingers caressing his hands as he lifts them from the dirt.

He puts the turnip on a pile of other dirt-caked vegetables and pulls out a small pocketknife from his jeans. He puts a gentle hand on Michiko's shoulder, and she turns around to meet him properly for the first time today.

              JIN
    Maybe hold onto this
    and just keep it on
    you all the time.
    Just in case,
    y'know? And to make
    you feel a little
    safer if you see him
    and I'm not around.

Michiko frowns and takes the pocketknife. Their bodies are close together as they talk.

              MICHIKO
    We're gardeners, Jin.
    We just plant things
    in the ground and
    enjoy ourselves out
    here. What am I
    supposed to do with
    this?

              JIN
    It's just in case, Michiko.
    Honestly,

                    I don't think he's gonna do
                    anything.
                    He's just trying to scare us.

                              MICHIKO
                    You said that.

A pause and Michiko breaks away, picks up some
turnips, shakes the dirt off, and puts them in
                    a wood basket.

                              MICHIKO (CONT'D)
                    I'm sorry,
                    Jin...this is just
                    fucking with me.

Her hands are caked with dark earth,
emulsified with yesterday's rain, a paste
clinging to the lines of her palms.

                              JIN
                    We'll be fine.

He looks at the trees surrounding their
treehouse home, extending on forever,
vibrant reds and yellows, and the sound
of Michiko's feet crunching on dry
leaves.

> JIN (CONT'D)
> The cauliflowers are gonna be good to pick soon. Before it starts snowing.

Jin sees something in the treeline, turns to look at it, realizes it's just a shadow, and takes a few breaths. The sound of Michiko's footsteps is in the background, crunching on dead leaves.

CUT TO:

INT. COUPLE'S TREEHOUSE - NIGHT

Michiko and Jin are in bed, their bodies pressed close together and fast asleep.

There's a sound that resembles a braying donkey outside their window. It's loud and drawn out, guttural, like keening. Painful crying.

This sound goes on for a while, and Michiko is the first to wake up. She opens her eyes slowly at first and furrows her brow. She quickly nudges

Jin, who groggily wakes up to hear the horrible braying sound.

Michiko's eyes are wide open now.

>   JIN
>   What is that?

>   MICHIKO
>   Sounds like an animal.

Jin turns around in bed to turn on the bedside lamp, painting the walls with a dull orange glow

Jin gets out of bed, and Michiko follows close after him, in a big shirt that works as a nightdress. He grabs the flashlight from out of the desk while the braying continues, long and drawn-out, making both of them tense.

Jin grabs the flashlight in the drawer while Michiko gets the pocketknife on their desk, and they walk over to a large window looking over their garden.

Michiko gasps, and she points at a large silhouette in the middle of their garden making the noise. Jin clicks the flashlight on and shines it over the figure.

They see, crouched on all fours, the naked man from the woods, braying like a donkey, using all his energy to do so. Straining his whole body with a red face and a thick neck, showing his veins off.

Almost looks like he's grieving, braying like a donkey, scaring Jin and Michiko, but all they can do is watch as the naked man continues braying and braying and braying.

                  MICHIKO
        Let's get him, come on.

Michiko leaves the window, starts storming off.

Right as she does so, the naked man stops his braying, stands up as fast as he can, and runs off into the woods again.

                    JIN
        Wait! Wait. He's
            gone.

He looks up at Michiko, who's standing by their ladder. She turns around, sits down cross-legged, and starts crying.

Jin sits down across from her and holds her in his arms.

Michiko finally sits back up and takes a few breaths. It looks like she's just woken up from a night terror.

                    MICHIKO
          What WAS that?! What WAS THAT?!

Jin holds her tight in his arms. He's shaking too.

                              CUT TO:

EXT. GARDEN IN THE WOODS - DAY

A pair of bird's feet, broken off at the ankles, cling onto a piece of log by their garden, the rest of the bird missing—just the yellow clawed fingers gripping tight to brown bark.

Jin walks up close and inspects the feet, Michiko close by.

                    MICHIKO
          Bird feet.

                    JIN
          Must've gotten eaten. Their foot
          muscles hold on because of reflex
          sometimes.

Michiko stares at the feet and yawns, deep rings around her eyes. It's obvious she didn't get any sleep last night.

She walks up close behind Jin and presses her body up against his and holds his hand.

                    MICHIKO
          You need to know
          I love you, Jin.
          I love you so
          much.

                    JIN
          I love you too, but
          stop. We're gonna
          be fine.

                    MICHIKO
          I think he put those feet there.

Jin stares at the feet again, pulls them
off, and tosses them into the woods as
far and as hard as he can.

                    JIN
          Just some unlucky animal.

Michiko's breathing quickens, panic
starting to simmer.

                    MICHIKO
          That's what he wants
          to do to us, it's a
          threat.

                    JIN
          We'll be fine,
          Michiko. He can't
          do anything to us.
          He's just some
          naked man. We have
          a knife. A couple
          of things,
          actually. We don't
          need to be scared.

                    MICHIKO
          I worry sometimes that he's
          sacred.

                    JIN
          What?

                    MICHIKO
          There's nothing
          wrong with that...I—
          I think I'm just
          tired.

Michiko shuffles away slowly, sits down in a patch of dry leaves, and puts her head in her hands.

The morning sun shines down on the pair of chicken feet, disembodied and laying in the dirt. Wind comes and covers the feet under a layer of dried leaves.

                                   CUT TO:

INT. COUPLE'S TREEHOUSE - NIGHT

Jin is woken up by Michiko grabbing his arm. It's dark in the room but her eyes are wide open. She's got the pocketknife in her hand.

                    MICHIKO
            He's here. I heard him.

Jin blinks, wakes up more.

                      JIN
            Where?!

He flips over and turns the bedside lamp on, the dull orange a spotlight on Michiko's panic.

                    JIN (CONT'D)
            In the garden again?

                    MICHIKO
            By the ladder. I can hear feet.

They both stare at the ladder leading down, nothing but dark shadow below the fourth wood step.

They stare at the top of the ladder for a few seconds before Michiko gets out of bed and walks to the entrance of their home. She stands above the hole and looks down.

She peers down for a few seconds more before her face changes and her eyes focus on something at the bottom.

              MICHIKO
       THERE HE IS! HE'S THERE!

She looks up at Jin, Michiko's face full of determination, before she looks back down and puts a foot down firmly on a ladder step.

                JIN
       Wait! What're you doing?!

              MICHIKO
       We have to get him
       NOW, Jin. Or he'll
       get us first!

She's already climbing down, only her head visible over the entrance now.

                JIN
       Wait!

Jin jumps out of bed and climbs down the ladder after Michiko.

EXT. GARDEN IN THE WOODS - SAME

Jin alights from the ladder, and Michiko is peering off into the dark.

                  JIN
    You saw him here?

                MICHIKO
    He was right there.

The knife in her hand is shaking as she moves her head around, trying to look for the figure in the dark. It's heavy darkness at this hour, nothing but the silhouettes of trees.

She sees something.

                MICHIKO
    THERE HE IS. THERE.

                  JIN
    I don't see shit.

She takes off running, and in a moment, is swallowed up by the dark of night.

                  JIN

                    MICHIKO!

Jin runs after where she went but already
loses the sound of her feet. He swivels
around in the dark for a moment before
realizing he's lost her.

He runs back to the treehouse, their
room glowing a dull orange in the
night, and he climbs back up the
ladder.

INT. COUPLE'S TREEHOUSE - SAME

Jin's head crowns over the entrance
of their home as he emerges,
climbing up the ladder.

Head sweating and anxious, he turns
around and yells when he sees the NAKED
MAN (50) sitting on their bed.

Naked Man has a face full of concern,
his eyes big, his face and demeanour is
innocent: sitting on the bed, trying
not to take up too much space.

                    NAKED MAN

>   Whoa! Hey! You
>   alright, man?
>   What's wrong?
>
>   JIN
>   Where is she?! Where did she go?!
>
>   NAKED MAN
>   Relax, guy! Who're you talking
>   about?
>
>   JIN
>   My wife! She—FUCK YOU.
>
>   NAKED MAN
>   Whoa! What's going on, man?

Jin runs over to the desk, and yanks a drawer clean out, grabs the flashlight inside, runs to the ladder, and starts climbing down.

The structure has changed, and he only ends up climbing back down into his own treehouse home.

He turns around and sees Naked Man sitting innocently on the bed again, body hunched over and trying not to take up too much space.

Complete silence in the room except for Jin's laboured breathing as he stares at Naked Man.

> NAKED MAN
> What's happening, man? You can talk to me about it if you need to.

Jin's eyes are massive, full of fear.

> JIN
> What's happening?! What's happening!!

He runs back to the ladder and climbs down, only to yet again climb down back into his own home, where Naked Man is sitting on his bed.

Jin sees Naked Man, and panic overwhelms him. Out of options, he runs at the Naked Man with the black flashlight in his hand, ready to bludgeon Naked Man to death with it.

With little effort, Naked Man grabs Jin and completely overpowers him, pushing him to the ground and incapacitating him with his weight.

Jin can barely breathe as he's being pushed to the ground. One arm is awkwardly splayed out, with his other arm held behind his back by one of Naked Man's hands.

Jin screams and tries to thrash. But he barely manages to move.

>   NAKED MAN
>   Hey, man! It's gonna
>   be alright. It's
>   gonna be alright.
>   You're just
>   panicking. It's
>   gonna be okay. It's
>   all gonna be fine,
>   okay? You're
>   alright. Hey, hey,
>   this is gonna pass.
>   This is gonna pass,
>   alright? Just hang
>   in there.

Jin keeps screaming until he runs out of energy. His whole face is red, and

when things are silent, his laboured
breathing is audible.

>   JIN
>   Okay...Okay. I'm good. I'm—I'm
>   not
>   panicking anymore. Get—get off
>   me,
>   please.

Naked Man sits above Jin for a second
longer before he nods his head and
gets off.

Jin immediately gets to his feet and
stares at Naked Man.

Naked Man has a face full of worry and
concern. The two of them stare each
other down for ten long seconds, the
dull orange glow of the bedside lamp
making them look sick.

Jin turns around and runs for the ladder
again.

He climbs onto it and climbs all the
way down, only to yet again end up in
his bedroom with Naked Man again.

This time, however, Naked Man is quiet and looks sad. As if something has happened. His eyes trail the ground with disappointment.

Jin stands by the ladder, unsure of what to do.

The sound of braying begins. Long and drawn out. Almost exactly like the first night. Like the imitation of a donkey, a painful crying and keening travelling through the night air.

Jin walks towards the window, where the sound is coming from.

He looks out and shines a light on the silhouette out in the middle of his garden where he sees Michiko, naked and on all fours, her face red with strain as she brays like a donkey at the top of her lungs.

                              CUT TO BLACK

Who Does What

"I feel like a gallbladder," John says.

He rolls in the grime of the floor, letting the floor stick to him in long black strips.

"Feel like such a fucking gallbladder," he repeats, rolling over and over and over until his body is covered in long strips of black tar.

"I can't barely even see," he says, putting palms over his eyes as if that's gonna let him see better.

"Stop," I tell him. "It's not even funny. I don't like this joke."

"It's not a fucking joke," he tells me. "I feel like a gallbladder. Like you know when a gallbladder's got too many stones? That's how I feel like."

I walk over to him, and long strings of tar stick to my bare feet as I walk towards him. I put a hand on him to make him stop rolling, and my hands are turned a deep black colour from the tar. "Stop."

"Touch my belly," he tells me, and with his hands, he scratches at his stomach until the tar is wiped away enough that I can make out his belly button.

"Touch it, please," he says again.

I put a hand over his stomach, and I lightly tap his belly button with my finger.

"It's like seeing god," he says, and I watch as his eyes move up to the ceiling, and tears start streaming down, making rivers in the tar that covers his face, cleaning some of the black gunk away.

"I know." I nod, and I keep tapping his belly button, and with each tap, he becomes more emotional, and he's making big sobs that rack his entire body, and I can feel his stomach vibrating from the sobbing.

"I'm just this. I feel good," he says.

"I'm glad," I say.

Now his eyes open wider as he looks up at the ceiling. "Oh, here he comes."

In the middle of the ceiling is a little mound of flesh with a small hole.

A small face protrudes out of the hole and looks down at us. The face is veiny, and the thing looks at us with large, grey eyes, and it licks its lips a lot, moistening itself so that its mouth is glistening. "Got two here, got two," it says.

John starts sobbing even more now, and he closes his eyes, and I keep tapping his belly button to comfort him. And honestly for my own comfort as well.

"I don't like this," I say.

"It's okay," John says. "He's a fan, just like you and me."

"Shhh." I say, staring at the thing in the ceiling. I can hear as it smacks its lips and its tongue keeps darting in and out, and I'm jealous of its perfect tongue, with the perfect amount of bumps, three of them. One big bump at the tip of the tongue, one slightly smaller in the middle, and if you look closely, there's an even smaller one at the back.

"I heard that," the thing says.

I shake my head. "He didn't mean it."

John, in his unsteady voice, sobs, "No. I meant it."

"Fuck's sake. John." I stop tapping his belly button, and his sobbing starts to immediately lessen.

"I knew it. I did. I just want to be close," the thing says.

"He's just a fan," John says, looking at me for comfort. "Oh, please…he's just another damn fan."

"I don't want you close either. Just stay where you are. Please," I say to the thing.

The thing squirms in the mound of flesh in the ceiling. The face moves around, and squelching sounds escape.

It squirms until it dislodges itself from the ceiling, and it smacks onto the tar floor, and it squirms a little on the ground too, until it rights itself on its legs.

The face is human, though pale, and is connected to a thick but small larval white body. It has no neck, and so when it turns its head, half the body has to move with it. It has small little feet, like black segmented toothpicks coming out of its body.

It starts to crawl towards John, and I get out of the way.

It has a very large and defined face, strong cheekbones, and a long chin.

It keeps smacking its lips together, and soon it reaches John. "I just want to be close," it says.

"I don't want this," John says, trying to move out of the way, but his back is now glued to the bottom of the floor, and he can only move in small inches.

The thing gets on top of his body, and with the back of its little larva body, it starts to bury itself deep into John's belly button.

John starts to sob again, and this time it's deep sobs that rack through his entire body, and I can see that this brings the thing comfort as it closes its eyes and smiles.

Soon it's embedded itself deep into John's belly button, all the way up until only the thing's head is visible and not the rest of its larva body.

"I just want to be close," it says.

And John just shakes his head and sobs, and I imagine he must be feeling more like a gallbladder than he ever has.

Strange Weather Ahead

Bodi's got a fresh joint in his hand and he's lighting it up while Trudeau talks about this coronavirus stuff. Trudeau's got a fresh new beard on trying to act like he knows what he's doing, saying the same sentence over and over again.

Stayin,selfisolate,don'tgoout,nomeetingswithtenormorepeople ,stayin,selfisolate,wait for the whole thing to blow over and be the congregation.

I look up at the TV. Big, white oozing light making me feel sweaty. I wonder why Trudeau suddenly got so religious.

"You think it's the end of the world, Bodi?" Mo asks.

"Nah," Bodi says, blowing out smoke and passing the joint, "Tim Hortons is still open, right?"

"S'posed to rain tonight," I say.

Mo blows smoke and passes the joint to me.

Stayin,selfisolate,don'tleaveyourhouses.

Mo shakes her head and laughs. "It's like there's a world-wide school shooter or something."

"You said it was gonna rain tonight, Tai?" Bodi asks.

"Yeah," I say, "s'posed to be a thunderstorm."

Bodi nods his head, takes a long drag of the joint. While everyone went and panic-hoarded toilet paper, Bodi went and bought over a pound of weed, enough to tide us all over till next season.

Mo shakes her head. "Fuckin' politicians sayin' that we weren't prepared. Fuckin' idiots. We've been prepared for a long time. It's just you that's blindsided by this," she says, pointing her head at the screen pouring bright light, Trudeau's face illuminated by a pixelated glow, making me feel like a toy soldier melting under the sun's delirious warmth.

"Nah, they knew," Bodi says, "they've just kept their fingers crossed and hoped it'd never happen is all. 'Cause what the fuck can you do anyway if you *do* know?"

"Prepare," Mo says.

"So what," I ask, "you think every politician oughta buy a pound of weed too? That your idea of preparing?"

"Just sayin' that Trudeau ain't any more prepared than we are, and the only difference between him and us right now's the size of his house."

There's the rumble of thunder outside like massive hollow trees dropping.

"Told you there's s'posed to be a thunderstorm," I say.

"Shut the fuck up about your thunderstorms," Mo says, taking another hit of the joint, the room starting to fill with slow sedentary smoke like dust motes under the rays of digital white light.

"Gonna be things coming in with the rain tonight," Bodi says, nodding his head. He stands up and walks off into the kitchen, comes back with a mug of red wine in his hand. "I can feel it already."

"Damn! You had wine here this whole time?" Mo yells, jumping off the couch and jogging to the kitchen.

More thunder off in the distance, and soon the sound of rain pattering on the ground and the roof of the house starts as Bodi presents the still-lit joint in front of my face, now halfway through, and he says, "You've barely had anything to smoke this whole evening."

Smoke everywhere in the room, three hours later, and Trudeau's been saying the same stuff over and over and over again: *stayinselfisolatedon'tgoout.*

The rain is coming down hard now, like static all around us, enveloping the whole house with a fuzzy sound.

We stay indoors and burn with bright light.

I look up at the computer screen and at my friends to see if they heard Trudeau, and they're oblivious, one of them lighting up a new joint, the other one grinding more weed. Mo is on her third mug of wine.

There's a knock on the door, three sharp knocks, and Bodi jumps from the sudden sound.

"What the fuck?" I say.

"Was that knocking?" Mo asks, sitting up.

We're all seated deep in the soft couch, half-digested by its fine cloth and unwilling to move. We're quiet until the person outside knocks three times again, hard and fast.

"Should we see who's outside?" I ask.

"Yeah, maybe they're in trouble," Bodi says.

"What if they're sick?!" Mo says.

"We should see what they need anyway. We'll talk from a distance."

"If he gets all of us sick..."

"You're not gonna get sick."

"Fuck it," I say, "I'll go see who it is."

I pull myself out of the couch and walk up to the door and open it to grey sky, pouring rain, the evening coming in, and with it, more tumoured clouds in the distance—lumpy, heavy, misshapen, gliding slowly through the air like bison about to break into each other.

There're birds scattered all through the front yard, probably about a hundred of them getting wet in the rain. All of them are pigeons. Grey and round, their circular eyes stupid and unblinking.

There's a pigeon hanging on the door, pecking on the glass.
"Pigeons!" I yell. "They were knocking."
"That a person?!" Bodi yells back.
"No! Come'ere and look! Buncha birds here."
"Birds?!" Bodi groans, jumping out of the couch and walking up to the door. He peeks his head out and shakes it, walking back to the couch. "It's fucked boys, this means it's fucked."
"What?" I say, looking at the birds and their fat bodies, plump from gorging on city scraps.
"Close the door before they start trying to come in!" Mo yells.
I close the door and sit back down on the couch, sink back in, deep into the soft fabric. Mo puts a mug of wine in my hands and Bodi passes another joint.

I'm awake now but don't remember sleeping. I look around and don't see Bodi or Mo. It's night out now, and the rain's really coming down.
The computer screen is still on, images of the virus, a circular thing like a chicken egg with a broken yolk swimming across my screen, bright white computer light making me sweat a thin film of liquid already solidifying around my armpits and melding my spine to the upholstery of the couch.
The computer screen switches to a scene of Italy, its streets empty. Nothing but wind and wild animals now. Wild animals in Rome, wild animals in Paris, wild animals in Kyoto, roaming the streets while people sing from apartments and make music.
There's a video now of a Chinese family way back at the start of this epidemic, setting their stuffed toys on fire, stir-crazy and

filled to the brim with cabin fever and burning to death in the end, apartment full of plastic fumes.

"You'll lose it watching shit like that," Bodi says from behind me, joint in hand, producing more smoke, watching the screen through the thick haze in the air, "everyone's going crazy."

"It's not that bad," I say, "where's Mo?"

"Under the couch," Bodi says.

"What? Why?"

"Crying. I think she doesn't want us to see her."

Mo's Indian, with her mom far off back home, and with all the borders closed, it's a tough time for everyone.

There's a rumble beneath me, and Mo pops her head out, her eyes all red from crying and some snot coming out her nose, and she says, "Found some twoonies at least!"

"You alright, Mo?"

"Just gotta cry sometimes, y'know?"

"Why'd you hide?"

"Maybe I'm not drunk enough."

"I never find twoonies…" Bodi says, "sorry about your mom, Mo."

Still raining, spring downpour. Maybe it'll wash all this shit away, mix it in with the mud, and take it down into the sewers and out into the ocean. Mo has sat back up on the couch and is blowing her nose. "I feel so lost out here," she says.

"Sorry about that, Mo."

793deadinItalyyesterdayashosipitalsrunoutofventilators.

Trump's face appears on screen now. White light's gonna melt us all down into each other, remove the seams between each other, and emulsify all of us into something smooth.

TheChinesevirus,verysevere,verybad,verysevere,verybad,bad, notgood,bad,virus,notgood,notgood,foreignvirus,fromfaraway,notgo odverybadverybadnotgood,faraway,just as vikings pillaged towns from far away, years ago, so too will this virus come to us and ravage our cities and leave us with many dead and with more trauma than we will know what to do with.

I blink.

Verybad.veryveeeerryyyybad.

His lips are drooping downwards, panic causing his whole brain to shut down...but where did all that Viking stuff come from?

Already Bodi has passed me another mug of wine, sweet and with the pungent smell of alcohol. Hopefully, there is enough here to kill all the microbes hanging on to the walls of my throat.

New video now, some infectious diseases expert on the screen, full suit, talking calmly to Joe Rogan, *thisvirusisreallyjustoneofmany,manyanimalswithstrangediseases,ma nymorediseasesstillincaves,waitingtoappearbeforeus.Indeerandcervi ds,thereischronicwastingdisease,waitingtojumpontous.*

"Turn the computer off, this is too dark," Bodi says.

"No!" I say. "We ought to know."

I'm watching their lips, opening and closing, waiting for some new nugget to reveal itself.

Five sharp knocks on the door, and this startles Mo.

"Who's out there, you think?" She asks.

"I can go look," Bodi says.

He stands up and walks up to the door, and looks through the window next to it.

"There's a guy with a knife out here," he says.

"What?!" I yell. "Someone with a knife?"

"Yeah, he's got a kitchen knife in his right hand. He looks like he's got some issues."

"What the fuck should we do?!"

"I think we'll be alright actually, he's just standing there. He's not really trying to come in," Bodi says, peeping out the window sill.

"That might be the guy going around stabbing Asians in Peterborough!" Mo says.

"There's a guy going around stabbing Asians?" I ask.

"Last I heard it was a Thai guy got stabbed," Bodi says.

"Maybe this is a different guy and he only stabs white people?" I say.

"Why don't you go out and check?" Mo says.

More knocking on the door, a little faster this time.

"Do you think maybe someone should just ask what he's doing out there with a knife?"

The computer screen switches now to an image of Bernie Sanders on the podium, yelling his stuff, *wewillfightforuniversalhealthcaretotheveryend.Itisahumanright.*

And he looks at me, eyes meeting mine through the camera, and he says, *don't you see the pestilence?*

"I DO!" I yell.

Mo laughs at this and says, "Well, then go and talk to him." She shoves me in the side and I stand up.

I walk up to the front door and peep between the curtains to look out the window and see this guy standing out there, scrawny with a crutch under his left arm. In his right hand is a kitchen knife, dinked-up and old looking. He's soaking up rainwater, his hair clumped up seaweed hanging over the edge of his forehead, and his clothes are a few colours darker with all the water.

"You want something?" I ask through the door.

"You guys got a little something to eat in there?" he asks.

"Yeah, but I think it's just for us," I say.

"But don't you see the pestilence?" he says, and the rain is out there coming down hard.

"Of course I do," I say, "it's all I've been hearing about."

"You won't let me in?"

"Why d'you have a knife in your hand?"

"To stab Asians with," he says.

"He's the guy that stabs Asians!" I call back to my friends.

"Well, don't let him in!" Mo calls back.

"Yeah, he'll stab us."

I turn to the guy with the knife and I say, "Unfortunately we can't let you in because you'll stab us if we do."

"You're all Asian?"

"Yeah."

"You brought this disease here with you people."

"None of us are from China."

"I'll stab all of you."

"We'll call the police."

"I'll stab them too."

He spits on our front doorstep and stands there.

"We're not letting you in," I say, and he doesn't say anything and stands at the front door, soaking up the rainwater.

"I hope you get sick and die," I say, and walk back to the couch.

"He's not leaving?" Bodi asks, handing me a joint.

"He'll probably get cold and walk off," Mo says, handing me a mug of wine.

I take both, gulp the wine down, and breathe the smoke in like it's oxygen. The doorknob jiggles, and I ask Mo to pour me more wine.

Sleep enters my body through my spine, and the next thing I know, I'm waking up to bright computer light and both Mo and Bodi are dead asleep on the couch.

Images of black body bags on the floor, piled up in a corner in Iran, and a news reporter saying, *bodiespiledupasIranfailstotakecontrolofthesituation.Somanypeopledeadand* she looks at me *this is more than any of us can handle.*

Years of endurance to get here? To reach this point, after working so hard. What a waste. The dead sleep and we endure where they cannot, and it is all we can do, endure, endure, and endure until we're kneeling and waiting for doves to carry us away.

The doorknob jiggles, but this tiredness covers my head and puts me to sleep.

When I wake up again, it's because Bodi's got his finger on the trackpad of the computer, and he's about to close the tabs off.

Sleep still in my head, I grab his wrist and say, "Stop, stop. We need the info."

"It's too much for me, Tim Hortons is only doing drive-thru now," he says. "I feel like shit hearing about all this stuff. It really does feel like the end of the world."

"It's the only way we'll *know*," I say.

"Tai…" Bodi shakes his head, "I'm exhausted. I can't take all this news."

There's the sound of glass breaking in the kitchen toward the back. Mo sits upright on the couch and says, "What the fuck was that?"

Bodi and I have our hands still on the computer, our heads pointed at the dark kitchen, the sound of heavy rain now clear through what must be a broken window.

"What's happening?" I say.

"Sounds like someone just fucking broke in," Bodi says.

We're all quiet watching the kitchen when we hear footsteps and the sound of a crutch clicking.

In a moment, the man that was outside with the knife appears from the kitchen and stands in our living room, still with a crutch under one arm and a knife in his other hand. He's got cuts and bits of glass sticking to him where he must've fallen through the open window.

He's staring at the three of us and we're just staring back at him.

He opens his mouth, yells, and charges at us as fast as he can, the crutch making clacking sounds on our wood floor as he runs at us, raising the knife to attack. Bodi and I stand up, getting ready to protect ourselves, when Mo slams into him from the side, her whole shoulder sending him completely off balance and into the computer.

There's a loud cracking sound, and the screen breaks in half. The man falls hard on his wrist and yells out in pain, "AOUGH, OHH. OHH…. It's broken! I can't move it, oh my god I can't move it."

The three of us stand around this man on the ground, his knife dropped far from reach, and he's got his face all scrunched up in pain, and we look at each other.

"You really fucked him up, Mo," I say.

"Should we call an ambulance?" she asks.

"Nah," Bodi says, "they're busy with this virus stuff happening."

"We oughta kick him out."

The guy starts crying now, his weak frame shaking on the wood floor, and Bodi sighs and shrugs. "We'll give him something for the pain and get him outta here. I think there's something wrong with him."

Mo kneels down to his face and says, "You can't just go around stabbing Asians, guy."

The man doesn't respond and just keeps crying.

Bodi comes back with a red solo cup full of wine. Mo helps get him back onto his feet, and I hand him back his crutch.

He's standing there still crying, not moving a bit, and so we start pushing him, and we push him out the front door.

"Fuck off and stop attacking people," Bodi says, giving him his cup of wine. We slam the door behind him and lock the door.

We watch him through the window as the pigeons return, congregating around his feet at first, and looking up and watching this man cry, all of them mesmerized by the man standing in front of our doorway, and soon there are hundreds of pigeons in front of our house, watching him, soaking up rainwater.

In a moment, the pigeons fly onto him, their little orange feet clinging to his clothes, and soon there are so many of them that their feathers hide the man's entire body, and he is just a giant mass of grey feathers, missing under their throbbing over-abundance, their bodies shedding feathers all over the ground through their collective friction.

They take off all at once, holding the man tight in their grip, and we watch as he is taken far off into thunder clouds. Bodi looks at me, shakes his head, and tells me that pigeons are dirty animals.

Hunger in the Heavy Heat

Heavy heat in the orange evening, hot enough that it's bending the white walls of apartment buildings off in the distance; concrete mirages; sunlight boring through the scalp making us feel delirious; sticky sweat clinging to my armpits and drying into a crust, and Mahram is smoking a cigarette and watching the cops down the street playing volleyball with the local junkie's severed head.

All the cops are in their blue swimsuits and laughing with rosy red cheeks as they toss Paul's head around, tongue out and eyes constantly rolling, and they sip beers, and I'm pretty sure I even see one in the distance cooking some ribs on a portable grill.

Mahram's got a new cigarette between his lips. "Man…honestly, that one cop in the back looks like he's cooking up something good. Hope it's giving you an appetite."

The smell wafts over with the wind every now and again, and I can smell the spices and rubs caramelizing on the meat.

Mahram takes a long drag of his cigarette, and I ignore what he said. "You think they're gonna start getting bothered by us staring?" I ask.

"Just wait. I'm already seeing some of 'em looking over at us."

One of the cops slams his knuckles into Paul's flying temple, and his head goes back over the net and down into the sand faster than anyone can react.

"Whoa! Damn!" One of the cops yells, laughing. "You ever thought of trying out for a team or something?"

"Dad used to want me to join the Olympics, actually."

"No shit!"

Another one chimes in. "I actually got pretty far into the whole process, actually."

"What you mean, you nearly performed in the actual games?"

"Yeah! Couldn't quite cut it, though."

"Bullllshit. They'd take one look at you and start laughing. What sorta sport you do?"

"Swimming…"

Some of 'em laugh. "Michael, you'd look like a fuckin' pregnant Bill Burr in a leotard if they ever tried putting you in a swimsuit."

Michael frowns, and his eyes catch ours staring at him and his friends, the two of us sitting on a concrete wall and watching them and the ocean waves in the distance, orange under the setting sun and full of sea-foam and sea-oak.

Micahel looks at his buddies, talks to them, and starts pointing over at us, and soon enough, all the volleyball-playing cops are throwing looks our way, and still, we're staring at them.

Mahram's smoking his cigarette, almost down to the butt now.

"What d'you think these cops do when they get home? I mean food-wise."

"I don't know. Microwave dinners, I'm guessing."

"I think they don't care. I think they sit by themselves and drool."

"What d'you mean?"

"Look at 'em now. They're starting to eat."

And Mahram's right: grill-cop's got paper plates and is handing ribs out to all the other cops, and now they start to dig in.

Mouths wide open as they chew into soft meat, and the juices and spit spill through their open lips to pool yet again on their plates or on the floor, mixing with sand and clumping the sediment together.

Meat jumps from their mouths as they talk and laugh among one another, chunky sauce glazing their mouths and glistening in the sunlight.

More of their eyes catch us staring at them, and they start muttering amongst each other as they stare back.

Five days now they've been playing with Paul's head, and we'd all been friends. Paul was a good simple guy who did too much meth, but still, he was nice, trying to quit and failing each time 'till we stopped hearing from him one day, and then one evening I get a call from Mahram, and he's crying and telling me they're playing volleyball with Paul's head, and we came out to the beach here and saw them bouncing Paul's head all over the court, eyes rolling and rolling and rolling, the whole time Mahram standing next to me, shaking with anger in the evening sun.

We're staring at them, trying not to blink, and finally, one of them tosses their half-finished rib away and walks towards us, prompting the rest of them to follow a few steps behind.

"Walk away," one of the cops says, "nothing to see here."

"Just watching you play volleyball," Mahram says, "what's wrong with that?"

"Move along."

One of the cops behind the main one, face shaking and turning red behind his aviators, yells, "He's watching us, Cole! Look! He's watching us!"

Another cop comes up behind this cop sweating and shaking and puts an arm around him. "Ned! Ned! Hey, shhh, it's okay, man, it's okay."

Ned breaks down and starts sobbing into the cop's shoulder. The cop cradles Ned in his arms, stares up at Cole, and says, "Fix this."

The two of them walk off the volleyball court and onto a bench in the distance, where Ned the cop continues sobbing and rubbing his eyes, big globs flowing down flushed cheeks.

Cole, the main cop, turns back to us, and puts his hand on the grip of his taser. "Leave now."

"We can watch you people if that's what we wanna do," I say.

"You fucking killed Paul," Mahram says, "where'd his body go?"

"There was no body."

"Oh! So, what, you just found his head?"

"Listen…we're just out here minding our business, so why don't you just go and—"

"You ate him!" I yell. "Hid his body in your bellies."

The cop pulls his taser out and points it at us. "Walk away now. Last warning."

The taser's in my face and I imagine those prongs digging into the skin and I look at Mahram and he nods and I know what needs to be done.

I grab Mahram's arm, pull his sleeve back to reveal the skinny arm beneath, open my mouth as wide as it will go, and bite down on his flesh as hard as I can, taking a massive bite out of his forearm.

Big iron taste in my mouth full of salt and Mahram barely reacts, and Cole the cop, in front of me, watches completely entranced, still pointing his taser at us, watching and drooling at the sight of this consumption.

Some cops behind him are starting to freak now. "What the FUCK?! SHOOT him!"

"Is he eating his fucking friend?!"

"Shoot the bastard, Cole! What the fuck are you doing standing there?!"

And more cops are headed towards us now, faces full of panic and with their tasers up, some of them watching Cole's entranced reaction, not looking away from my full chewing mouth. I take another massive bite of Mahram's forearm, leaving two gigantic bite marks that go all the way down to the bone, and Cole the cop finally snaps out of his trance and shoots the taser right at my chest, and it's nothing but white light in my body and my arms shooting down to their sides and everything in my body tensing up with nothing but white light and white heat going up and down setting me on fire, and the next thing I know they've got my arms handcuffed behind my back, and I'm looking around and seeing Mahram on the ground too, two massive bite marks in his arms, bleeding bad, and they're handcuffing him, and I watch officer Cole's face and see nothing but hunger.

Diphenhydramine, for Allergies and Other Things

Benadryl™ Benadryl© Benadryl®.

Marley's high off the stuff again, diphenhydramine, or DPH, and I can tell soon as I walk into her apartment: staring off at a wall, sitting so long she's gonna get bed sores.

"Marley," I say, standing at the open doorway of her room. She's usually pretty neat and tidy, but she's been searching through all her drawers for something, and stuff's all over her room—crumpled clothes and bottles of water. There's a single dim orange lamp in the corner, shading the room with dull yellow and orange, and she's staring at the wall.

"Marley," I say, walking into her room and tapping her on the shoulder.

"JESUS," she jumps back, her eyes wide and her pupils dilated so big I imagine them growing out into the whites. "Don't *fucking* touch me."

"Chill the fuck out, Marley. It's me."

"You just came in? When did you come in?"

"I just did. Just walked in. You didn't hear me knocking? Musta been out there five minutes."

"I'm tripping out right now, man," she laughs, "you think I'm listening to the front door?"

"Yeah…I can tell," I say, "how much you take?"

"700 milligrams, man…" she brings her hands up slowly and curls her thumb and her last two fingers in for a weak peace sign. "The 700 cluuuub. You know it."

"700?! How long you been tripping for?"

"Mmmmmmmm…two hours now? How the hell'm I s'posed to know anyways. Din't you hear? I'm on 700 baby. 700 cluuuub."

"Yeah, you said that."

"When did you get here?" she asks me.

"Man, you're really fucking tripping."

"You were here just now already, y'know…"

Her eyes go blank and she stares off into space.

"Marley?" I say.

She grunts and keeps staring at the wall.

I see the stuff on her desk, a few packs of Benadryl allergy medication with most of the neon pink pills popped. They just make you a little sleepy when you take it for allergies, but up the dose into the 300 mg range and higher and you get high off the stuff. Diphenhydramine is full-on delirium, and it fucks with your body hard and fucks with your memory, and all everyone ever says is how it'll give you dementia in your 30s, and it's on the pharmacy shelves and abundant in the kids' section of Shoppers Drug Mart for when spring comes along.

I guess it's been daily use at this point for a whole year now, and she's always out of it. She's always been curious. She looks for all the legal stuff 'cos drug dealers scare her, and the dark web was too complicated and it ended up with her buying a bunch of bitcoins off a website called bitcoins.com and wasting a lot of that money because she used a website called bitcoins.com.

So she did legal stuff like salvia, DXM cough syrup, which is also on the pharmacy shelves, and huffing things like nail polish remover.

She's pale as fuck. Black, greasy hair clumped up together about to make dreadlocks and looking like inky spaghetti noodles.

We've been friends for a long time. Before, her exploration in the weird legal stuff never really changed her, but then she started getting heavy into the pink pills ever since her dad died—and what a nice guy, too. I'll come by and see her, check in on her all the time, but the Benadryl's basically got her shut indoors most days.

"You look like a zombie, Marley."

"Get the fuck out of here," she says, turning to look at me with sudden clarity, "you came in here just to call me out or something? Fuck you."

"Relax."

And I see she's breathing hard and fast and is staring at me, confused, with her eyes wide open. "What're you here for anyway."

"Well shit," I say, pulling out my phone, "I got a new phone, bitch!"

She's quiet and stares at me.

"It's the new Google one. Check it out it's even got this crazy voice recognition thing."

I bring the phone higher up between us and say, "OK Google, how do I get a friend to take a shower?"

"Here is an answer from Quora," my phone says, and it shows a list of results from the web.

"Fuck you," says Marley.

"Chill out. It was a joke. But also actually, fucking go shower. Or wash your face, 'cos I can smell you from here."

"Shit," she says, pointing her eyes down, "It's been a while for sure. But I can't freaking remember the last time I woke up and the last time I…" she looks off into the distance and spaces out, and I can see it in her head now, all this scraggly brown dirt, full of sudden images of webpages and being somewhere else—maybe in a shopping mall, maybe standing by the bus stop. One time I was driving her home and she realised suddenly that we were in a car. She tells me she can be in two places at once.

"Hey… you zoning out on me again?" I say.

"NOOooo…." she says, standing up slowly. "Y'told me to wash my face. I heard."

She stumbles towards the bathroom and opens the door. I walk over to where her table's shining silver with popped aluminium tabs of pill packaging. I look in her trash can and it's overflowing with more silver wrapping. "This isn't even cool, Marley. At least meth or heroin's got some street cred, but you're hooked on fucking allergy medication."

A rusty squeak and the white noise of water gushing out her faucet begins, and I can hear her splashing water on her face.

"Why do you even like this stuff, man? Doesn't even look like you're having a good time."

She's silent except for the sound of running water.

"You heard what I said?" I call.

She's quiet still, so I walk to the open bathroom door to see her staring mouth-open at her mirror. She jumps when she sees me and looks back at herself, and the features of her face wrinkle and form hundreds of long dark lines across her skin, her dilated eyes iridescent as the backs of flies.

"OHHHH, I'm dead!" she yells, shaking her head.

"What?"

She's got her fingers gripped on the supple lip of her sink.

"Oh, Koj, I'm dead!" She puts a hand to her heart, and she shakes her head. "It's not beating!"

"Marley, relax! You're not dead. I'm talking to you right now."

"Ohhhhh, ohhhhhh!" She's shaking her head faster now and she runs to me and she's left the faucet on full heat and full blast and there's drops of water spraying out the sides of the sink with hot steam rising, and she grabs my arm with her long nails and they're so long they sink deep in my skin and she pulls my hand over to her chest to feel her heartbeat.

"That fucking hurts, Marley!" I yell, trying to yank my hand back.

Marley's breathing hard and she's so high that she loses her balance when I pull back, and she swings towards me with the momentum, loses her grip on my arm, and falls to the ground. There's a loud smack as she hits her head and she starts to convulse.

I gasp and crouch down to hold her head up. Her whole body's covered in spasms and her eyes are all up in her head.

"Marley! Marley! Oh shit. Holy fuck."

I pull my phone out and toss it on the floor, and in my panic, I ask, "OK GOOGLE, HOW DO YOU—WHAT DO YOU DO WHEN SOMEONE IS HAVING A SEIZURE."

"I'm sorry, could you repeat the question?"

"Shit!" I yell, and I'm about to ask again when the spasms begin to die down and her muscles stop tensing.

"Marley, are you alright?" I ask, and her eyes are open again but she looks confused, and the next thing I know she's got her arms wrapped around my waist and she's buried her head in my stomach, sobbing, and she isn't really here, hasn't really been here for a long time, missing under the pink viscous waves of delirium, but I will be here for her anyway, waiting for her to return whenever she does.

Nourishing Itself On the Walls of Our Home

Late night and I'm standing in the garden behind my house, plants all around me, dim greens and saggy leaves under the pale fluorescence of a single white bulb collecting moths above my back door.

There is a snail here eating my basils, their fragile white flowers swaying gently under the weight of the snail's brown shell. Its mouth moves like a blanket over the leaves, and I pluck it up by its shell and toss it over the fence, where I hear it thud against soft grass.

There's a movement to my right, and I turn and see a figure crouched a little off in the distance, around the corner of my house, the round shape of a human body, the white light of my garden barely reaching its feet.

I walk up closer to the figure, and my eyes adjust to the dim light enough that I recognise it as my mom. She's crouched down on all fours, her knees on the dirt, and her arms crossed over her head like she's hiding, black hair a waterfall over her wrists.

"Mom?" I call.

She gasps and looks up, still crouched on the ground. "Oh, you're awake."

"I came to check on the basils," I say, "something's been eating them and I wanted to catch 'em. Just some snails, though."

"Mmmm…I doubt it," my mom says, "it's whoever's living in the hole."

"The hole?"

She lifts an arm up and points at where the wall meets the ground, and I see a hole large enough to crawl through, leading into complete darkness.

"The hole just appeared today, but it's been here for a while."

"How do you know that?"

My mom looks down, her whole body starts shaking, and I realise she's crying. "I think it's what killed your father."

"What do you mean?" I ask, staring now at the hole, unable to control my breathing. My dad had starved himself to death many years ago, refused food until his skin bruised easily and blossomed with purple hues, and soon enough he was nothing but a skeleton wearing loose skin, and then he died on the couch one morning.

"I don't know exactly," my mom says, "I'm just sure. I know what it did. I came here, wanted to get rid of it, maybe…I don't know, confront it somehow, but then I got here and my body tensed up and I couldn't do it."

The hole is there, forcing my eyes to its pitch-black centre, and then I see what looks like movement, a slight shuffling noise moving deeper into the hole, and I look at my mom. "Let's head back into the house."

I put my arms around my mom's shoulders, smaller than I remember, and she says, "I don't feel safe."

"It's going to be fine, mom. I'll figure it out somehow."

She looks up at me. "Why did the hole appear today?"

"What?"

"It's been here all these years, hiding underneath the house...why now?"

I frown, can't think of anything to say, so I squeeze her tight with my arms and say, "It's gonna be okay, mom, we should at least try and sleep."

She nods and says, "You go ahead and head in. I don't feel comfortable going back in yet."

Back in the house, I see her eyes are still puffy and red from crying before the hole. I tell her I love her and head back to my room.

I'm in bed, trying to fall asleep, and all I can see is the hole in the side of my house. I keep trying to think of something else but I end up back at its entrance, and I find myself crawling into the hole headfirst, going deeper and deeper into cool, dusty earth. Deep enough that I can't see anything, and soon it's getting cramped enough that I can't turn my body around anymore and have to go further, and I can feel the earth squeezing my chest from the top and bottom and only getting tighter with each movement.

I reach the end of the tunnel, completely dark. I only know it's the end because my face has brushed up against hard rock and dirt. I try pushing my body backwards but nothing happens. I feel to my left and right for a passageway but find nothing.

"Help," I call, and the word leaves my mouth without me thinking it. I take a breath and can feel the panic building up in my chest and radiating into my bowels, and I fight back the urge to call out a second time.

I try wriggling backwards again and realise my thighs are pinched in by the top and bottom of the tunnel and I'm completely stuck. It becomes too much and my heart is beating so fast I can feel it thumping against the tunnel walls, and I start pressing my arms against the walls trying to do something, punching the dirt until I feel a soft felt blanket and open my eyes to see that I'm still in bed and covered in dirt.

Grey morning light glows through my curtains and I barely got any sleep. I get out of bed, wash off all the dirt on my body in the shower, head to the kitchen, pour hot water over ground coffee beans and watch black liquid pool over brown sediment, and that hole is still in my head, pitch black going deep under the house. If I go down there, I ought to bring a light.

The smell of coffee brings me back, and I pour it out into my mug, take a sip, and realise I burnt it, making it taste like bitter dirt.

I pour out what's in the pot and boil a new one.

Steaming new mug in my hand as I walk out into my back garden again to see that all my plants are still being eaten. There are big circular holes in my basils, and the leaves of my tomato plants look like someone has hole-punched through the leaves, all of them starting to brown and wither already.

I walk up to my tomato plant and see there are still two fruits going from green to red, plump and untouched, so I pluck these off the branch and save them in my pocket.

I walk back around to where the hole is, now in the morning light, and see my mom still crouched over it, not having moved the entire night.

"Are you okay?"

My mom nods. "It could be worse."

"Why don't you come back into the house?"

"How could I?"

"Why not?"

"We should have left when your father died, Hyun."

"I like this house. It's our home," I say, and already I see my mom staring down, not wanting to look at me.

"We should have left instead of sitting here in his absence all day…for years. How many years now?"

"It's a good home," I say, "I love it."

She looks down and then at the hole. "I won't go in. It's not safe."

I sigh and stare at her, her hair getting greasy in the humid air.

"I don't want to leave here until we get rid of this thing under the house. We owe your dad that at least," she says.

I nod and look at the hole, as dark as it looked when I was here at night.

"I'll cook breakfast and bring it out for you," I say.

"Thank you," she smiles, "I'm so hungry."

And I head back into the house and wish she'd just come back in.

Turning the stove on, all I can see are the big purple splotches that went up and down my dad's arms as he became more and more emaciated, skin becoming so soft that pulling a band-aid off peeled skin along with it like low-quality notebook paper.

The hot pan becomes hotter, and the metal of our electric stovetop turns the colour of incandescent lipstick as I pour oil in and crack an egg to hear the sizzle of gooey translucence turning solid and white.

Days after our gorgeous Doberman dog died, my dad had started staring at his food, just sitting at the table and staring at his plate for hours, unmoving. I used to think it was guilt over having run over the four-legged family member, but now mom's talking about this creature living under the house, and all I can see is that hole when I close my eyes.

The eggs have started to brown nicely, so I sprinkle in salt and pepper, plate the eggs, chop up some basil leaves salvaged from the garden, already looking droopy and wilted, and sprinkle it over the eggs. I fill up a glass of water.

I bring the plate of eggs out to my mom, and when she sees and smells the eggs her eyes go wide, and soon enough she's scarfing them down in the heat of the sun getting brighter and hotter as the day begins.

Soon enough, her plate is empty except for the leftover oil, a sheen over white ceramic. I hand her the glass of water and she puts it up to her lips and gulps it all down until it's gone.

"Thanks so much, Hyun. I love you so much."

"You should really come back in, Mom."

She shakes her head and stays in her crouched-over position next to the hole.

I pick up her used dishes and bring them back in. I pull the same ingredients out I used for my mom and cook myself breakfast.

I sit down at the dining table with a full plate of eggs and basil. I shake some salt and pepper over it, cut a piece off, put it in my mouth, and as soon as I start chewing, my appetite disappears.

The taste of the egg coats my mouth and I feel completely full with just one bite.

I keep chewing the eggs in my mouth, and they turn rubbery like chewing gum. I swallow what's in my mouth and feel it going down into my stomach, and I feel like I've just eaten a massive meal.

I know my body needs more, so I spoon another piece of egg into my mouth and feel the need to vomit. Something in my body tells me I've had enough but I keep chewing, so nauseous that I'm scared to swallow.

I push the eggs down my oesophagus, and my body is telling me to stop, and all I can feel is the grease coating the back of my throat, coating the bottom of my tongue, and I can barely look at my food.

I sigh, put a hand over my tender stomach, and think about my father starving himself to death and feel anxiety strong enough that I force another spoon into my mouth and chew, chew until it's a soup in my mouth and thick against my tongue, and I can't bring myself to swallow it, so I grab a paper towel and spit it out.
    I stare at the food on my plate. I pull plastic wrap over it and tell myself that I will finish eating all the food by the end of the day, and see again dark purple spreading up and down my father's skin, his own body eating itself for the sustenance he couldn't provide.
    Something must be done about the creature in the hole.

    I go up to my room, open a drawer, and pull out a keychain flashlight—small but with a bright white cone of light. I take a breath and decide that I'm gonna find the creature tomorrow afternoon.
    Evening comes sooner than I thought it would and I try eating two more bites of my eggs and instantly feel full to bursting again, and so I pull the plastic wrap over my food, fat dewdrops of condensation hanging over the eggs, some of them dripping off and pooling in yellow eggs, and put the plate back in the fridge.
    I feel wetness in my pants pocket. I stick my hand into the pocket, feel seeds, and remember the tomatoes I plucked this morning. My fingers wrap around soft tomato skin, and I pull the fruits out to see that they have hundreds of perfectly circular holes that have perforated throughout the walls of their bodies.

A feeling of disgust goes up through my whole body, and I toss the tomato in the trash and wash my hands with soap three times over, and all I can see are all the tiny holes leaking clear-red tomato juice.

I boil a bowl of instant noodles up for my mom, the smell of chicken broth warm and nauseating, and I watch as hard noodles soften and sink. I chop some bok choy up and toss them into the pot and watch their green hues deepen before turning the heat off. I pour it all out into a bowl and bring it outside for my mom, who is still there, crouched by the hole, head down.

"You want dinner, mom?"

"Yes please," she says, "mmm, I can smell it from here!"

I set the bowl down next to her and she's slurping the noodles up, full of hunger and drinking warm soup, teeth crunching over fresh bok choy.

I stare at the hole next to her, imagine myself entering: headfirst is the only thing that makes sense, and I wonder how far this hole goes.

Soon enough, my mom's finished her dinner, and all that's left in her bowl is sediment from the broth.

"Have you eaten yet, Hyun?" she asks.

"No," I say, "but I will when I'm back inside…you're not uncomfortable out here?"

"Not half as uncomfortable as when I'm inside the house," she says.

I nod, kneel down next to her, hug her, and she holds me in her arms.

"I'm gonna go down into that hole tomorrow," I say, "I'm gonna get rid of whatever's down there."

My mom nods. "I've been hearing something moving. Every few hours, I can even feel it shifting sometimes if I put my head on the ground."

"So it's still down there."

"It hasn't left the hole so far."

I nod, take a deep breath, and crouch down to hold her hand for a second before I take her dishes and walk back inside.

I put the bowl under the sink and watch the grey uneaten sediment at the bottom being washed out.

Night comes, and I'm lying in bed and unable to sleep, tossing and turning, sweat turning humid under the blankets, my armpits turning sticky and my legs wet with condensation, so I pull the covers off and take my shirt off and toss them on the floor. I touch the sides of my body and feel the sweat, and then notice my rib bones with the tips of my fingers. I run my fingers along my chest and feel the bones protruding, pushing against skin.

I get out of bed and walk over to a mirror to stare at my skin, and I feel like I can see the anatomy beneath my skin and am disgusted. A complete lack of hunger and yet I feel as though my body is starving so I run downstairs, pull the egg out of the fridge and see that it has also been left with hundreds of tiny perfect holes. I decide that my body needs this food badly, and so I rip the plastic wrap off and scoop the eggs into my mouth with my fingers.

A complete feeling of nausea spreads down from the bottom of my jaw and into my neck and down into the pit of my stomach and I can't help but stop chewing.

I take a breath and lean on my fridge, bite down on my eggs two more times before I try swallowing it.

While they slide down my throat I realise this isn't going to work, and I run to the bathroom and can only reach the sink before it all comes back out as a chunky pale yellow congealing in the drain of my sink.

I turn on the faucet and wait for the food to flow down, but all that happens is the water rises and stays there, full of floating, half-eaten eggs.

Exhausted, I decide this is too much and go back to bed.

Morning comes full of dark grey clouds in the sky threatening to rain and rain and rain. I grab the flashlight from my drawer, pass by my bathroom, see the sink still stuck full of water and ignore it, walking to the kitchen to grab a chef's knife.

My stomach feels full and heavy, and just looking at my fridge makes my belly feel wrong, as if something is already there and taking up all the space.

I walk outside and go around to the corner where my mom is still crouched over.

"Good morning, Hyun," she says.

"Morning, mom."

"Looks like it's going to rain,"

I look up, stare at the clouds, almost black with how heavy they are.

"Looks like it," I say.

"Are you gonna make breakfast for us?"

"I'm dealing with that creature now. Before it can do anything to us like it did to dad all those years ago."

"Oh…" my mom says, looking down at the hole, "be careful, Hyun. Get rid of it quick and come back as soon as you can, okay?"

I nod, standing now over the entrance of the hole.

I take a breath, crouch down low, and start crawling into the hole headfirst.

In a moment the visibility is gone, and it's all just a dark hole in all directions before I reach down to my pocket and pull out my flashlight. I click it on and a narrow cone of white light shines down the tunnel, revealing dust motes floating through the air.

I crawl forwards, my elbows and knees doing most of the work, the only sounds my clothes dragging across the dirt floor.

This continues for what feels like many long minutes until I hear and feel some movement up ahead: a shift in the ground. My heart's beating against the tunnel wall and I continue onwards.

I keep crawling forward and I shine my light up ahead to see a sharp-turning right, what looks like a complete ninety-degree angle. I decide to keep crawling onwards with my knife held tight in my right hand.

I reach and turn the corner, move my head around, put my flashlight up, and see it.

A man's naked body with the head of a Doberman dog. The bottom of the dog's neck is long and fused to the start of the human body's neck, making its head protrude to a much taller position than it should, the skin where it has fused scabbed over and scarred.

The front part of my torso has gotten stuck around the sudden angle of the tunnel and the sight of this creature makes me want to scream as loud as I can, call for help, for someone to drag me out of the tunnel, but the chords in my throat have lost all strength, and though I can still breathe I am unable to make a sound and am left staring at this animal-man.

The animal-man stares at me, watches me as I try to scramble backwards, using my arms to try to squeeze myself back through this corner, but my waist is firmly stuck.

The animal-man, on all fours, crawls up next to me and holds my face with its dirt-caked hands. It forces my head up, makes me stare at its head, and I finally see that it is our dog, killed by my dad's messy driving all those years ago. I try to bring the knife up and realise my hand is caught between the space of the tunnel wall and my hip, just shy of being able to do anything.

"I love you, and I love your father dearly. Your mother too," the animal-man says.

I try to rip my head away from its hands but it holds me firmly in place. "I woke up after I died that day," the animal-man says, its voice quiet and soft, "I woke up under the house, just a head. I couldn't do anything, and I barked and barked and barked, and howled for days, and no one heard me, and I was alone, only a head here under the house."

Fear in my whole body and I'm still trying to push the knife through the thin space between my body and the tunnel wall, but my knuckles are stuck firmly in place.

"Soon enough I felt nothing but hunger," the animal-man says, "and I couldn't do anything. I could only move my eyes, and in the end, there was no light to see. I stayed here for a long time, but at night I would dream, and I would dream of our family, all of us living in the house as something happy and normal, and I would see your father by the dining table, unable to eat his food, and I would wake up in the dark the next day feeling nourished and satisfied. I had no choice. Dreaming brought me to the living room and always to your father who did not eat, and each time he did not eat, he fed me fully."

The animal-man holds my face, caresses my nose and my ears, touching every feature, and it says, "I started to see in my dreams your father growing weaker, gaunt, and it made me sad to see him wasting away, and I could do nothing about it. One day I woke up and felt a body beside me. I knew through instinct who it was, and I stayed with this body until it became obvious it needed heat. Instinct alone pushed me to chew at his neck, and I chewed until I had gotten through everything, and I moved myself with the muscles of my jaw until I pushed the bottom of myself to the stump of his neck and felt the warmth of his body, and the love. Especially love."

Nothing but the urge to scream and panic in my whole body as I realise it has taken over my father's body, that I am here before him now. I feel the tunnel walls tight around me.

I finally manage to push the knife in my right hand through the tight squeeze of the tunnel wall entirely, and it slices into my father's thigh. The animal-man howls and flinches backwards, and I manage to squeeze more of myself through and am about to stab the creature again when I look at my father's body and see that it is fat and healthy. His skin is thick, has muscle beneath it again. The deep dark purple bruises that spread across his body at the slightest movement are gone, replaced by healthy tissue.

I start sobbing, tears filling up my vision and pouring down, and overwhelmed, I drop my knife and cry, staring at the ground, not daring to look up at what has happened.

"I love you, I do, I love you as much as I used to," the animal-man says, coming close to me and putting its arms around me in an embrace, but I am disgusted, and I push it backwards, still crying, unable to say anything. I start crawling back the way I came.

I squeeze through the angle, better than I did before, and stare behind me and see the animal-man isn't following.

Water trickles down from the tunnel entrance, and as I get closer to the surface, I hear rain.

Cold water now flowing down against my face and soaking into my clothes, causing me to cough with so much of it flowing down my mouth, when I finally break through the tunnel entrance and into the rainy day, heavy grey clouds pouring above me, and my mom crouched by the tunnel. I'm soaked with water and she asks me what I found down there but my voice is still too weak and I cannot speak.

Despicable Blue Pig

    Another cop, another bad day.
    This one's harassing some sucker going too fast down the road. Man must've been going five or ten over, and still this pig's gonna come in with his schlong all full of blue and red lights like some clown's popsicle dick, and he's writing this guy up a ticket.
    Dude's sweating like crazy, too, I can see him from this porch, and it's the middle of fucking winter. Makes you think he's probably got some sorta paraphernalia up in the back or something, and all you can do is hope the pig doesn't catch on and bring a dog out to catch whatever baggie of drugs this sweating dude has.
    Or maybe he's just got a sweat gland issue. Who knows with people these days. But from the look of anxiety on his face, it looks like he's got something in the car he ought not to have. The cop gives him a ticket and lets him go.
    Winter afternoon and the sun's coming down like a white-yellow laser beaming straight into the eyes, and everyone's all squinting. Snow's all over the road, too, so all you get is just these giant rays of sunlight shooting up all over the place. Gonna give a man sunburn.

    Some dude comes walking up to me on my porch. He's wearing a full outfit of plaid. Red and black for his shirt, and black and white for his pants. He's got short hair, cut unevenly. Looks kinda dopey.
    "You Macon Norm?" he asks.
    I look at him for a bit. "Nope."
    "I think you're lying."
    "What?"

"You're Macon Norm."

"I look like Macon Norm to you?"

"Yeah."

"What's Macon Norm supposed to look like?" I ask.

"I dunno, never seen him."

"And you know I'm Macon Norm?"

"You have a Macon Norm vibe."

"I'm not Macon Norm."

He nods and inches closer to where I'm sitting out here on the porch. "Sure. Sure...Macon."

"Macon Norm sounds like a white name," I say. "Do I look white to you?"

"Don't be fucking racist, anyone can have any name," the guy says.

"Well, I'm not Macon Norm."

"What's your name, then?"

"I'm supposed to tell you? Just came up here outta nowhere, and you want me to tell you my real name?"

"Well, if you're not gonna tell me a name, you sure as hell sound like Macon to me."

"Fuck you here for anyway?" I ask.

He comes up close to me. "To kill Macon Norm."

"What?"

He pulls out a long chef's knife, a little dinged up and slightly rusty.

"You plan on stabbing me with that or something?" I ask.

"Hell yeah, after what you did to lil' Ginger Tom, I'm gonna kill you 'till you're dead."

"Well, you better get the fuck off this por—"

He lunges at me with the knife, and I fall back in my wood porch chair, which crashes behind me. This plaid man is on me in a moment and is bringing the knife down on my body, and I can feel it stab into my chest and belly a total of three times before I push him off and bring my fist down on the right side of his face in a neat right hook.

He gets back up dazed, but the knife is still in his hand.

I look down and see my shirt's overflowing with blood, and I've been stabbed bad. There's red all over the snow, and this sunlight's bleached everything white and is making that blade of his gleam like some sort of sacred object from God.

The cop from across the road must've seen the commotion and all this bleeding, 'cause he's come over now, and he's got his gun out, and he's pointing it at plaid man, and he's yelling all his pig words, "DROP THE KNIFE AND GET DOWN ON THE GROUND."

"Get the fuck outta here!" I yell back. "This shit's between me and this guy over here."

"We're gonna get you to a hospital soon as possible, sir, don't worry. Just put pressure on those wounds."

"Fuck you!" plaid man yells back. "You know how long it's taken me to *find* Macon Norm?!"

"I'm not fucking Macon Norm, asshole!"

"PUT THE KNIFE DOWN!" the police officer yells.

I run up to this here police officer and sock him right in the nose so hard I can feel something cracking and crunching on my knuckles, like a walnut breaking up in his sinuses, and he falls down, face scrunched up and full of pain and red running outta his nostrils, a big river of iron.

"This shit is *our* business, asshole," I say, kicking the cop in the side.

"Yeah, asshole." Plaid man says and kicks the cop on the other side.

The plaid man looks at me, and he says, "You're not so bad, Macon. Used to be that I thought you were some fucked-up douchebag."

"I'm seriously not Macon."

I must be bleeding bad, 'cause my clothes are all soaked in blood and twice as heavy, but something about punching that pig in the nose has got me feeling like I've just taken a hot shower.

Deep Green Gravity

"Ambil tu… 那个 zui," my jia gong says, pointing in the direction of two blue cooler boxes that are huddled together with some snacks, fishing rods, and rolled-up tents for our camping trip. I open the coolers up and see that they are both filled with plastic water bottles of Nestle® Pure Life®, all old enough that most of the plastic looks dented and worn out, with some of the labels peeling off and leaving behind a sticky residue that collects dust and turns fuzzy.

Jia gong means grandpa in either Hokkien, Cantonese, or Hakka. I'm not sure, honestly, and just like my grandma, whom I have only ever known as popo, I don't know what his actual name is.

I grab some red and orange bags of prawn-flavoured crackers that are huddled around some of our other camping equipment and one of the blue coolers and start hauling it towards my jia gong's shitty red Perodua Kancil. The cooler is heavy, and I can hear the bottles inside bumping against each other and sloshing as I haul it up into the back of my jia gong's car. The weight of the coolers brings the ass of the tiny car a little closer to the ground, and I see that cramped into the corner of the trunk is jia gong's ancient hunting rifle resting on and compressing a small blue box of surplus ammo. Guns are a rare sight in Malaysia, and jia gong is the only person in our family to have a license. I look at the smooth, well-oiled metal a second longer before slamming the trunk door closed.

I pull my phone out of my pocket, tap the screen, and see my battery is at 97%, which should let it last two days at least if I don't use it too much.

Just the two of us now, driving down winding Klang roads, moving further away from the city, palm plantations an ocean of homogeneous green, and their husky trunks lined up in massive uniform rows that go on forever on either side of the road as my jia gong's foot stays steady on the gas pedal, the air conditioning of the car old and only ever blowing hot outside air in at this point. My jia gong clicks the A/C off and the speedometer immediately jumps up 15 km/h, and I can feel sweat collecting and sticking to my nose.

I look out at all these stumpy palm trees, some of their green leaves shrivelled into ashen grey and brown dryness under the intense afternoon swelter of the Malaysian sun, high up in the sky and causing heat mirages to distort the air around us, turning cars in the distance into indistinct wavy colours and making the road ahead look wet.

Further in the distance, where the jungle has yet to be cut down to be turned into palm oil, is the rainforest. Thick leaves of many types, broad or fern-like, bushy and competing for space, trees struggling to get past the canopy, their branches wrapping around each other as they strangle one another and breathe in sunlight. Crowning above some patches of green canopy are massive sheer walls of white and grey limestone.

Jia gong coughs a few times, clears his throat, winds the window down and spits a fat ball of phlegm out onto the road.

His English sucks. Barely speaks any of it, which is too bad cause that's really all I speak well. His main language is Hakka. Our whole family is Hakka, but really only he and two of my cousins know how to speak it. Useless language anyway since you'll never find someone dumb enough to commit to learning it in Malaysia.

He's the only old Chinese guy I know who talks to other Chinese people in Malay. His Malay's perfect; better than his

Mandarin. Probably how he ended up being a cop all those years back. Probably that plus being a veteran of the Malayan Emergency.

A massive truck with an open bed of pigs rolls down the road beside us, large enough and with enough speed to feel its vibrations from inside our car. Each time its fat wheels go over uneven road, I can see the smooth-skinned pigs in the back hopping and bumping against each other. Its exhaust pushes out a constant stream of thick black smoke that travels up and dilutes in the humid air.

"Wahhhh," my jia gong laughs, looking at the smoke pumping out of the exhaust pipes, and he points to make sure I know what he's talking about, "很漂亮 hor? Cantiknya!"

Only a cop would find car exhaust pretty.

I look at my jia gong, a thin man with liver spots that run up and down his arms and brown pigment pools around his forehead in big sheets of discoloured skin. His hair is there, but…it kind of looks like it was gathered together by uncoordinated crows.

He thinks I didn't understand him, so he turns his whole head to look at me, and he points again at the truck now much further ahead, its black smoke the most visible thing about it. "Very pretty," he says.

"Choking hazard," I say.

Jia gong laughs at this. "You speaking, very nice."

Soon the large swathes of palm plantation on either side of us give way to random nature growing over itself. Thick vines and their groping leaves wrap around electric poles and their wires, covering rubber, plastic, and rusting metal under thick green.

My jia gong makes a wide turn off from the main road and onto a dirt road, which forces him to slow down as the car dips and rises over crumbled rocks and uneven earth. Above, the trees begin to shade us from the intense afternoon sun while allowing tiny spots of yellow sunlight to sieve through the gaps between the leaves to polka dot the dry ground.

    My mom used to tell me stories about my jia gong. I'd barely seen him growing up since he'd gone off to Indonesia to work after my popo died when clotted blood caused both her kidneys to burst.

    My mom loves him. She says he's a good father and then tells me about all the times he'd come home drunk, still wearing his blue policeman's beret, and how he'd line all his kids up against the wall and force them to recite the multiplication table.

    Mom always talked about him as a loving father who would play songs like My Prayer by The Platters on the ancient brass gramophone he used to own, but then also how he'd get head-swaying-drunk and then go out with his massive mutt dogs and harass people late at night, knowing no one dares to challenge a cop, yelling 'till most people in Sungai Buloh knew who my jia gong was and what he was about.

    My mom grew up real poor with my jia gong, and he'd make traffic stops to accept bribes all night 'till he got a barely livable salary that fed a family of six.

    Mom tells me he used to dote on her. That she was his favourite out of all the other kids, would sneak extra chicken wings to her under the table. She says I look a lot like him.

    Jia gong rolls up onto the most even patch of dirt road under thick shade. He twists the key in the ignition and the car stops vibrating. He turns to look at me, smiles, and pats the back of my hand twice. "Here!"

    "A lot further than I thought it was," I say.

He just smiles and nods at me.

We get out of the car, and immediately I'm hit with the high-pitched drone of cicadas and humidity collecting against my skin, forming an extra layer of damp stickiness.

Jia gong takes in a deep breath of air 'till his chest is puffed up, and then he lets it all out as a long sigh.

"Fresh," he says.

I smile and nod at him. It's true. The air here is so different. A thousand different smells coming together to form the distinct smell of thick rainforest, wet earth, and humidity mixing together with the occasional sweet or rotting scents of blooming flowers. Far in the distance, I can hear the rushing water of a waterfall, and I can see jia gong with his head angled, listening for the sound, too. Every once in a while, there is the far-away, throaty hoot of some animal.

Jia gong takes a few steps towards a thin tree by the edge of the dense jungle before he bends down low to inspect the base of its trunk.

"来, 来," jia gong says, motioning to me with his finger to come close, "see." He points at an etching at the bottom of the trunk, and when I crouch down next to jia gong and look closer, I see that someone has etched Chinese characters deep into the wood that read "一直有一只观鸟". I have no idea what the words mean, and I know jia gong is illiterate.

Jia gong digs deep into his pocket and pulls out a small silver compass. He flips the cap open, holds it out flat on his palm, and waits for the red needle to settle before looking up towards the dense rainforest. He walks up towards what seems like impassable, thick greenery; plants with fan-like leaves that are razor-sharp poke out around each other, but jia gong lifts them aside by the base of their leaves to reveal an indistinct dirt path that leads into deep jungle.

"We here," jia gong smiles at me before standing up with a creaky "aiyah…"

Jia gong walks back to the car to grab some of our gear, and I'm still here, by the Chinese characters etched into the trunk of this tree, and I'm staring at the words, written with almost perfect handwriting with something that has bitten deep into the wood, and then I see some movement within one of the characters, and so I move a little closer to look better.

There is something curled up within the empty space of one of the characters: a dull orange and black bug is sandwiched deep inside, and I can see its body moving slightly from side to side. I look even closer, and I see that it can't be a single bug, but it is actually a massive amount of tiny insects close together. I can barely see them deep inside the etching, but suddenly they move all at once, and it gives me an itchy feeling in the back of my head, and I have to stop looking.

I hear jia gong grunt and the scraping of plastic on metal, and I look over to see him trying to pull the cooler out the back, so I get up off the ground and run over to help him out, though the sight of all those bugs moving together makes me want to scratch at my neck and the grooves of my elbows.

I run up next to him and lift the cooler from the bottom before setting it on the ground.

Jia gong smiles and pats me on the shoulder before he reaches further into the trunk, grabbing his hunting rifle and slinging it over his shoulder and holding the box of ammo in his right hand.

Already my sweat is causing my shirt to stick tight against my skin like a wetsuit, turning the yellow fabric a shade darker.

I reach into the trunk, grab a backpack with both our rolled-up tents and put it on. I feel a stinging, itchy sensation by my forearm, and I look down to see a black and white striped mosquito with its red, engorged abdomen still drinking when I bring my hand down and turn its body into a thick paste of black and red against my skin. The humidity causes its body to stick to me even as I grab a dried-up leaf off the ground to wipe away at it.

Jia gong bends down and lifts the cooler on one end, "来, 来. Come tolong."

I lift the cooler up from the other end, and together we walk past the etched tree and to the hidden trail jia gong showed me.

Jia gong steps over the fan-like plants that cover the dirt trail, but I don't see some of the leaves, and I can feel their thin greenery cut into my calves and ankles, causing tiny cuts that bleed slightly and scab over in minutes, and I accidentally bring my foot down and squish the plants flat.

Nature documentaries always show the rainforest in bright neon green colour correction, but here we are greeted with a dark green that covers everything in its heavy shade. The cicadas and their constant drone blend in with the sound of distant rushing water, and in the distance, some animal jumps from tree to tree, causing branches to creak and the loud brushing sound of so many leaves being pushed against each other.

Jia gong and I follow the winding dirt trail, stepping over massive tree roots that extend far beyond where the trees are, roots that shoot out from the dirt and rest on the ground before reentering the earth a few metres away, hard and sturdy, many roots larger than my forearm.

More mosquitos land on my body. I slap at the ones that are trying to land on my legs and arms, but a few itchy welts are already rising on the back of my hands and on my left knee.

My whole body feels heavy with the weight of humidity as we continue along the trail, and the cooler full of water bottles sloshes between us as the occasional bird calls out from the branches above.

The sounds of water get closer, and its smell is in the air, fresh and cool, creates its own atmosphere in the jungle, and soon enough, we see the stream, perfectly clear, running between rocks and over smooth sediment.

I can see jia gong smiling as he watches the water.

We start walking along the damp sides of the stream, which grows stronger and wider the further upstream we travel, with miniature tidepools hidden behind larger granite rocks that cause different currents to move between each other to form spirals.

Some water seeps in through the sides of my shoes, and I can feel my socks getting damp, and I look at jia gong with his flip flops on, purposefully stepping into deep pools of cool water.

The rocks start to turn slippery with algae, and jia gong says, "Care, yeah? Care."

"Mm." I nod in agreement, and we continue with slow caution.

Further up, mini-waterfalls have started to appear, along with deeper streams and rocks thick with silky algal bloom.

Jia gong motions over to the sturdiest and driest patch of ground, and we set the cooler down. He pats me on the back and says, "So good."

He now wades into the stream until the water is touching the cuffs of his brown cargo shorts. He bends down, cups water in his hands, and splashes it onto his face before he cups more water and takes deep gulps.

He smiles at me and motions me over, "Clean. So fresh...tak boleh beli air ini."

He laughs at his joke and I smile back and nod. The walk has made me thirsty, and the water is so clean I can see all the way to the bottom sediment.

I wade in beside him and splash cool, refreshing water against my face before cupping water in my palms to drink.

It tastes clean and the humidity in the air around us feels lighter.

I look at my jia gong now as he takes in a deep breath of air and starts wading back to solid ground, and I can't help but wonder which jungle he'd been in during the war.

Growing up, my mom had told me the story of when he'd fallen into a pit trap set up by the communists, and how his whole platoon had left him for dead. And then, a few days later, he had somehow managed to climb back out and rejoin his team.

The Brits had given him a couple of medals for his bravery and valour, but we've since managed to lose them, probably thrown out by accident with a bunch of my popo's stuff after she died.

I wonder if jia gong had killed communists in the war. I wonder what he would have done if it was popo in Batang Kali when British troops came in and massacred everyone with automatic gunfire, rubber-tappers just like my popo.

If he could, he would probably tell me the Japanese came in and slaughtered fifty thousand ethnic Chinese across Singapore and Malaysia, plenty of Indians and Malays too. Now look at how small Batang Kali is. Another burning village. Well, maybe he wouldn't say any of that. I don't know him that well. It's the stuff my popo used to say. She always talked about the Japanese and all those hidden places in the jungle where bodies pile up.

I cup more clear water in my hands and take another long drink, feeling the coolness spread down my chest before wading back to solid ground with jia gong.

We continue following the stream uphill to its source, can hear the rush of water get louder, constant white noise a background static that blends together with the loud droning of cicadas to make one massive wall of sound.

More, smaller waterfalls appear before us the higher up we climb, the water now much more aggressive and filled with foamy white force.

I bend down by the stream, cup my hand in, and take a drink of water. As the water goes down my throat, I taste, in the back of my mouth, the subtle and foul smell of rot.

This makes me spit, and jia gong turns, sees my face and laughs. He comes back over to me and pats me on the back as I gag and spit over and over again to get the taste out of my mouth. I try to find the words to communicate with him. "好像…uhm…macam ada rosak sudah."

Jia gong laughs. "Rosak? Air terjun boleh rosak?"

"Yeah…macam…rotten. Busuk sudah."

Jia gong just shakes his head, cups a big handful of water and drinks deep. He smiles at me and says, "Sedap!"

I spit one last time to try to get the aftertaste of rotting meat out of my mouth before we pick the cooler up and continue our trek to the best waterfall near the top.

Wild orchids begin to appear on either side of the stream as we continue. Fat, colour-saturated petals extend from long vines as if trying to breathe the gentle spray coming off the waterfall, and soon there are hundreds of them on either side, in colours of purple, red, orange, light blue, and pink, mixed with the deeper greens of their vines and leaves, and their sweet syrupy fragrance becomes thicker, almost overpowering in the air as we continue on.

And then I notice it: rot, beneath the flowery smells, but still there. Mixing together with the humid heat and fragrant pollen to turn into something pungent and nauseating, impossible to ignore and lingering in the back of my throat, sweet and sour.

A big, black and iridescent carpenter bee moves from orchid to orchid, covering itself in yellow dust, totally uncoordinated in its messy flying.

The earth beneath us starts to plateau, and the rock formations that form miniature waterfalls begin to even out into a single calm stream as we continue.

The smell of rot is heavy in the air now, inhabiting the back of my throat, beginning to overpower the sweet smell of orchids that hang around us from their long vines, and then I look up and see something half-submerged in the stream up ahead—the large body of a mammal, grey and black.

Jia gong looks up and sees this too, and I watch his body tense up as he pays close attention to this thing laying in the water up ahead. The stream flows gently around its body, causing its hairs to float under the current like clumps of seagrass. The animal's neck is bent so that its body hides its head.

Jia gong bends down low, picks a rock up and tosses it so it lands with a heavy plop next to the large animal.

It doesn't react, and jia gong relaxes a little bit and starts walking up to the animal's body. I follow close behind him, and I can see now that there are flies buzzing all around the animal, and the smell of rot intensifies the closer we get to it, the still air allowing the thick, sticky smells to linger in the afternoon heat.

We get close to this animal now, and I see that it's a dead water buffalo, a big guy with large horns. Its large, dark brown eyes stare blankly, with the lower half of its face submerged in water. Flies buzz around his big curved horns and land across his bloated body to clean their mouthparts, lay eggs beneath the fur, and feast. It's easy to tell male water buffalo apart from their slightly smaller, shorter-horned female companions.

"Wahhh," jia gong says, bending down to look at the buffalo, unfazed by the rot, and all these flies buzz up all at once at any slight disturbance in the air, and their feet land against the backs of my ears, and the top of my head, and I swipe away at them knowing they've touched all that dead skin.

He smiles up at me and raises both his arms for scale, "Besarnya! Big."

I think about having drunk from downstream of all this rot, and it makes me nauseous enough to get me dry heaving. Not looking, I step into a deeper part of the stream and get my shoes wet. Cold water seeps in, and my socks absorb it all, and I can feel the bottoms of my feet squeaking against the soles of my shoes.

Jia gong pats my back and says, "No sick, no sick. Badan kita lagi…strong!" He laughs, flexing his thin arms so the sinewy muscles show past his now loose skin.

"Two days die ago," jia gong nods, bending down to put a hand on the ox's head. The hair all over its body is thick with grease, and I can see clumps of ivory-coloured fly eggs stuck close to its skin. Water passes through its slack open mouth, and its blocky teeth create tiny, new currents that flow back into the main body of water. Its body leaks dark liquid into the water from its underside.

I think about how to put the words together before I say, "Macam mana dia mati?"

"Mana saya tahu?" Jia gong laughs, walking around the animal's dead body, looking for what might have killed it.

"I think kena sick," he says.

Flies buzz up from the ox's dead body to fly around my head and land against my skin, where I can feel their fuzzy feet tickling the hairs on my arms.

A metre-long piece of black driftwood floats downstream towards us, and I grab it as it floats by.

I come around to the dead ox's side and poke at its skin to try to expose its belly as maybe whatever killed this thing did it from beneath. I manage to lift the loose skin up and we are both immediately greeted with a massive, silky, and dark green algal bloom growing from its underside.

There is so much thick algae underneath this ox that it looks like a hairy green rug has grown out of its skin, almost enough to hide its legs entirely. Clumps of the stuff break off from the disturbance and begin to float downstream.

A large bit of algae brushes against my ankle, and this startles me enough that I drop the driftwood, causing nasty rot water to splash back up in my face.

Jia gong laughs as I go back into a spitting fit, and I wade upstream of the ox's body as fast as I can to splash cleaner water against my face.

Jia gong wades through the water to where I am and pats my back as I keep trying to spit this sour taste of rot out of my mouth.

"I think break time," jia gong says, nodding his head and pointing a little further down to a small, dry clearing beside the long stream of water.

I nod, and together we pick the blue–white cooler box up again and wade our way towards the clearing.

We step out of the water and are greeted by tall, husky tree trunks with massive broad leaves at the top. Thick green vines wrap themselves around the trunks of trees, and various parasitic ferns and their lush greenery bloom from the sides of trunks, all of them fighting for more sunlight and swaying in the humid breeze. I pat the phone in my wet pocket, pull it out, and tap the screen on to make sure it's okay. The battery is already at 72%, and I hadn't even been using it.

"Okayyy," jia gong nods, "here good place go camping." And with that, he pulls his backpack off and starts to unfold the neatly packed navy blue tent.

He moves fast and doesn't ask for my help as he pushes metal stakes into the ground and ties the tent down to them, knotting string together with practised fingers. I'm untying my shoes and trying to peel them off my feet. They're soaked, and my feet feel vacuum-sealed to my shoes.

By the time I've got my socks off, jia gong has already set up most of the tent and is about done tying the top tarp that keeps the rain off.

"Saya boleh tolong?" I ask.

"Habis sudah loh," jia gong laughs, pulling a knot taught before sitting down on a flat rock and sighing.

He points over at the cooler box sitting next to me. "来, zui."

Him asking for water makes me realise how thirsty I am, and I pull the lid off the cooler box and see all those bottles of water sitting on top of each other, and I toss one over to jia gong, which he catches.

I grab a bottle for myself, twist the cap open, bring it up to my lips, and immediately taste bitter, burning alcohol.

I swallow the little bit that I let through my lips and wince, and jia gong's sitting across from me, laughing so hard he's falling off his rock and looking down at his water bottle in awe.

"Wrong loh!" he laughs.

The alcohol I swallowed tightens my throat and dries my mouth out even more, and I grab another old plastic bottle with most of the Nestle® Pure Life® sticker worn off, and I uncap it and immediately smell more vodka.

"Wrong loh!" jia gong laughs, and he's laughing so hard he's barely making any sound, just shaking his body and giggling till his face is red. He raises his bottle up to me in cheers and takes a long sip.

Humid heat sticks to my skin and dries my throat out even more, making it feel like I'm not breathing in enough oxygen.

I think back to the start of the day, and I remember the second blue cooler box and feel panic blooming through my chest.

"Wrong one?!" I yell, opening the top of the cooler, uncapping more bottles of water and only smelling alcohol.

"Takde hal pun! No problem, no problem!" Jia gong laughs and waves his hand out in a big arc, pointing to the stream and its gentle flow, but the smell of that rotting ox is still in the air, and I know it's just downstream, though from here thick tree branches cut into our line of sight to obscure its body. "Mana you tengok pun ada air," jia gong smiles.

I look to the stream, and it feels like the inside of my throat is wrinkling with dryness. I take another sip of some vodka, and all the liquid does is burn against my lips and the back of my tongue with bitter strength, and it makes me feel like I'm not getting enough air with all this humid heat sticking to my skin like plastic wrap.

Jia gong brings his vodka bottle up to his lips and takes another long sip. He looks up at me and says, "You buat bagus saje."

I can't think of the Malay word for thirst, so I say, "Yeah, but…I'm so thirsty," unsure if he even understands any of that.

"If thirsty, then…" jia gong says, standing up and walking over to the stream, cupping water in his hands and taking a long drink. He sighs when he's done, looks back at me, and goes in for more.

My mom told me about how much he used to hunt. He'd go deep into the woods and shoot wild boar, bring it home to eat for at least a week, and use every single part of it: braise its meat and turn its guts into soup. She told me about how his aim was perfect—would shoot a bunch of squirrels to skin and eat at home, and they'd all be shot straight through the eyes.

Apparently, he isn't just a good shot but is also an excellent butcher, and mom has told me stories of how he'd butcher his wild boars out in the jungle and then bring the meat into town all tied up in bleeding plastic bags, and he'd hand the bags over to my mom who was still a kid and tell her to ask the nearby convenience store to put the meat in their fridge since our family didn't have one. Mom tells me about how the store owners hated this but would never talk back to a cop.

My mom told me how he'd even shoot dogs, monkeys, and bats and bring all of it home to eat. I'd tell her that's not good, that things like bats carry disease.

We didn't know anything back then, she'd say, and rice is only so filling.

When he's done drinking from the stream, he walks over to our gear by the tent, rummages through his backpack, and pulls out a big bag of puffy prawn-flavoured crackers.

My throat is sore with dryness, and so I walk over to the stream and see the ox's body further down where we came, its head now angled in my direction.

I bend down, cup water in my hands, and take a long drink. It washes the harsh bitterness of the vodka away, but even though this ox is downstream of the water I'm drinking from, I can still taste the savoury fermentation of rot in my mouth.

Something is stuck to my teeth: it feels coarse and inedible like hair, and I dig my fingers around where I feel the hair and pull it out to see that it looks like the same green algae that were growing out from below the ox.

I fight back the urge to dry heave and flick the algae back in the water.

"You tak lapar?" jia gong asks, lifting up his opened bag of prawn crackers, a smiling cartoon prawn over the silver plastic packaging, and jia gong's fingers look pollinated with its orange flavouring while he chews with his mouth open.

I nod my head, and he tosses an unopened bag of prawn crackers over to me. I rip it open and see all the puffy crackers inside like styrofoam packing peanuts. I pluck one out and eat it.

Salty crispy prawn flavour spreads across my tongue, and I can feel the rough texture of the cracker rubbing against the roof of my mouth.

I'm about to eat another one when I feel all that salt drying my mouth out again. I look back at the stream and figure I'd rather not have to drink from this water so soon, and plop the cracker back in the bag and curl the top up.

Jia gong crunches down on another prawn cracker before putting his own plastic bag away.

He shakes his head at me, "Not good food." before he moves over to where all his gear is, leaned against the tent, and he grabs his hunting rifle. "Make good food."

On May 13, 1969, riots broke out across Malaysia, and ethnic Chinese and Indians were targets, with Chinese and Indian homes being burned down and then of course more violence when Chinese and Indians started attacking Malays who had nothing to do with the riots. Mom told me about how he'd gotten everyone to board the house up and hunker down while jia gong spent the next four days up on the roof with his rifle.

The Malaysian Government brought the army in, implemented a curfew, and began a shoot to kill order for anyone outside their homes. There are many stories of the army shooting people at their front doors, along with accounts of people not knowing a shoot to kill order was in effect.

My mom likes to say a lot that animals probably look at us and laugh at all the stupid things we kill each other over, and I always wanna tell her that male langur monkeys will kill baby langur monkeys that are not theirs.

Jia gong pulls his compass out, watches as the needle settles, and starts walking deeper into the jungle.

That alcohol I sipped has me feeling a little lighter, the ground less solid than it was a few minutes ago, and I don't wanna be here all by myself, so I roll my wet socks back up, squeeze my feet back into my still-soaked shoes, and run after jia gong before all this dense greenery hides him from my line of sight.

I run up close behind him, watching his rifle sway on his back, and I feel a pinching sensation on my ankle. I lift my leg up to see a massive black ant the size of a child's thumb has clamped down hard with its mandibles on my skin, making it sting.

"Fuck," I breathe, and reach down to pull it off.

It holds on tight, and when I tug on it hard enough, there is a quiet popping sound. Its whole body comes off between my fingers, but its head remains stuck and clamped down on my ankle.

Wind blows through, and all the leaves brush against each other in a massive flurry of brustling sound, and I can close my eyes and see waves crashing over the shoreline.

Jia gong doesn't notice me lagging behind and keeps walking as I brush this ant head off my ankle, and then I notice the sound of leaves being shifted beside me and what sounds like a man clearing his throat, and I turn to my right and see not too far off from where I'm crouched is a wild boar digging its nose into the ground and uprooting the earth around the base of a massive dead tree with a large, lush, dark-green parasitic fern growing out of its brittle middle.

The boar looks up at me, and we both make eye contact.

"Hmmmmmmm..." the boar hums, and it is a nice, consistent note.

I look up at jia gong and see that he has walked even farther off, but I don't want him to see this boar, because I know he'll try and kill it.

The humming gives way to a gurgling cough, and I turn back to the boar to see it's got its mouth open and is dry heaving. Its whole body vibrates with the effort of trying to cough something up, and then I finally see some slimy, dark green and blue iridescent thing slide out of its throat, past its blocky teeth and yellow tusks, and plop out onto the disturbed earth the boar was digging through.

The boar looks at me in the eyes once more before it turns around and runs off as fast as it can.

"You berak ke?" Jia gong calls, realising how far I've lagged behind, "kalau mahu berak cakap saje lah! Nanti saya jalan sampai Kuching macam mana?"

I have no idea what he just said, so I call back, "Ada barang here."

"Har? You dah berak?"

"Ada barang!" I yell louder, and I can hear his feet brushing against plant leaves as he walks back to me.

I can't stop looking at what this boar puked up, and I grab a brown, dried-up leaf off the ground and wipe away at thick saliva covering this dark, iridescent thing.

I wipe away at the saliva until I realise I am cleaning it off feathers and that the boar has puked up a small bird.

Jia gong comes up next to me and squats to have a better look at the soil when he sees the bird in my palms, and I can smell the vodka on him. He picks the body up with his bare hands, and now I can see its dark green head as jia gong lifts its black beak off its iridescent chest.

"Ohhh," he says, lifting a wing up to inspect it, full of thick, sloppy saliva. He then brings his fingers up to the birds head, and with his thumb, he lifts an eyelid to reveal a bright red eye like a cranberry with a hole in the middle.

"这是..." Jia gong says, thinking about what the bird is called, and then he says, "这是 ah-sian g-lossy starling."

"Oh…" I say, looking at this dead bird, about the size of jia gong's hands.

"Bird like this," jia gong nods, "tasty."

"Eurgh," I say, sticking my tongue out, which makes jia gong laugh. "Fuck no."

At this, jia gong shakes his head and drops the bird body back to the loamy earth the boar had dug up. He stands up, looks at me, and says, "你不知道饥饿."

I don't know what that means, so I just nod and follow after him as he stands up and walks deeper into the jungle.

Thick heat causes time to distort, making it feel like we've been walking for hours, and we've been baking beneath humid shade as the bright white glare of afternoon sun cuts through the canopy, and the heavy heat causes sweat to pool in my clothes and stick against my skin. The air is nothing but deep green humidity, and it is heavy enough that moving takes effort, and it constantly feels like I'm trying to breathe through a thin film of water. The sound of constant cicada drones and birds chirping and squawking in massive numbers makes it so I still see large green leaves all around me even when I close my eyes.

Jia gong doesn't pause, the rifle on his back creating a distinct line of sweat the length of the gun, but he barely seems to care.

My mom's always told me about the love jia gong has. I've been told the story a hundred times now of how once as a kid, my mom had been balancing on the lip of a massive, empty clay pot, and how too much weight on a single step had caused the whole thing to topple, and she had hurt her leg bad enough that she's pretty sure she broke it. Jia gong had known exactly what to do, and the next thing she knew, he'd gotten her whole shin wrapped in a splint with two pieces of bamboo tied together with cheesecloth, and then her leg healed like nothing had ever happened.

I must have been at least sixteen or seventeen the first time I'd met him properly, after he'd come home from Indonesia. He came home with so many gifts and soft toys and Jakarta fridge magnets for the whole family, and we'd celebrated with a big green pandan-flavoured cake full of cheap candles that dripped pink wax onto the smooth green surface, and we celebrated with so much tax-free alcohol from the airport.

"Wah!" Jia gong gasps, looking up at a tree branch, and he becomes hushed as he points at what he's looking at, "You see? You see?"

I follow what his finger's pointing at, and I see it in the branch: a large Asian glossy starling, at least twice the size of the one the boar had puked out. It opens its beak and calls out once, a high-pitched chirp.

I can feel my stomach starting to hurt from hunger, and jia gong pulls on the string of his rifle and holds the weapon in his arms. With his index and thumb, he grabs the bolt and chambers a round. Metal slides against metal and components click into place, and the moment he the round is chambered, I watch as the bird flies off and lands on another nearby branch.

"Tsk." Jia gong tuts, his eyes searching for where the bird landed, and I point over to where I see its black back feathers, now on a higher-up perch.

Jia gong pats my back and starts stepping through dead leaves, trying to make as little noise as possible.

I follow after him, can feel the layer of dried-out leaves get thicker as I follow jia gong to a better vantage point.

Jia gong walks over to a large, smoothed-over granite boulder, fuzzy with green moss and hardened orange lichen. He gets behind the boulder, rests his rifle against the rock, and moves it around for a second until it feels stable.

I crouch down beside jia gong. From here, I can almost see the bird fully, though leaves cast shadows across its body that help camouflage its iridescent green feathers against the bark of its tree. Its full back is towards me from where I'm sitting.

Jia gong looks down his sights and adjusts his aim.

I plug my ears with my fingers and look up at the bird on its branch when I see it move, and I expect it to fly off, but then I realise it's turning its head to look around, and as it does, I can clearly see that the bird's head is different now—no longer the tiny head of an asian glossy starling but the much larger head of an elderly woman with long black hair.

I gasp, am about to yell at jia gong not to shoot when I feel the shockwave of his gun go off and the sound of its massive explosion ringing through my body even though I plugged my ears.

We both watch as the body of the bird drops past the tree limb it was sitting on and becomes the much larger silhouette of a woman's body falling against and snapping tree branches before thudding on the soft jungle ground.

Seeing this makes my limbs feel far away, and an intense feeling of dread makes me aware of how hard my heart is beating.

Jia gong lifts his head off the rifle. His eyes look confused. He reaches into his pocket and pulls out his plastic bottle of vodka, about halfway finished already, and he takes a long sip. His hand is shaking as he recaps his bottle, and he runs a hand through his bird-nest of grey hair to try to calm himself.

"Bad…" Jia gong says, pulling the bolt of his rifle back and smacking its frame to get the spent bullet casing out, "must go now."

He slings the rifle back over his shoulder and stands up.

I've never seen him get so panicked before, and it scares me. "What was that?!" I yell, and I can feel dread building and calcifying in my body.

Jia gong doesn't say anything. He pulls his silver compass out and waits for the needle to settle. Sweat builds and drips off the ridge of his nose, and I feel how intense this static heat is. It builds on top of our sweat and insulates us in sticky warmth. Even when wind blows through, it is warm, wet air. The droning of cicadas is starting to make me feel nauseous and off-balance.

My arm itches and I scratch at it, feel the risen skin, and realise something bit me and I didn't know.

As soon as the compass needle settles, jia gong breaks into a fast walk. The alcohol makes it so he's stepping through thick bushes and thorny branches with no reservations, and I can see his thighs bleeding slightly from random nicks and cuts.

I follow after him and ask again, "Apa tu?"

He's still silent, walking so fast he's almost at a jog, and so I ask again, "那个是什么?"

He turns around with massive eyes and snaps, "How I know?!"

He takes another rushed step forward, where his foot lands awkwardly on a large protruding tree root and causes his ankle to roll and almost fold in on itself, and jia gong gasps and falls sideways.

I rush over to him and see his face—hundreds of deep wrinkles creased in pain, and his teeth clenched tight in his open mouth.

I look down at his ankle and see that it doesn't look horrible but is already starting to swell and redden.

"Aghhhhh…" jia gong breathes, trying to move his leg and wincing at the pain.

I put a hand on his back and say, "Is it bad?"

Pain turns into anger on his face, and he glares at me. "Bad! Bad! Very bad!"

"Can you stand?"

He doesn't say anything and tries to sit in a more upright position, and I can see him flinch anytime something causes his foot to shift.

"We're close, right?" I ask, thinking about where we set camp. It's gonna be a long walk through a slippery stream and uneven earth to get back to the car, and thinking about this sends a fresh wave of panic through my sternum.

Jia gong doesn't say anything, and he tries to stand back up again. He's got a palm flat out on the ground, and his face turns bright red, and I can see lumpy veins appearing on his forehead from the strain of trying to stand.

I come over and wrap an arm around his back to try to prop him up on his injured side, and he gasps and winces hard as I lift him until he's standing.

With his free hand, he reaches for his plastic bottle of vodka, uncaps it with his thumb and index, and takes a couple of big gulps that leave the bottle almost empty.

He recaps the bottle and puts it back in his pocket.

I look down at his ankle and see that it has started to swell into a big, red, taught balloon.

"Ready to walk?" I ask, looking down the same jungle path we must have taken earlier. Massive broad green leaves and thick ferns and vines and orange lichen and clouds of gnats spread out in the air around us. It feels like even the air pressure here is different. It takes so much more effort to move, and I feel weighed down by some hidden gravity.

    I look back to jia gong for an answer and realise he's crying. Tears stream down his cheeks, and he wipes them away with the back of his dirty hand, and it turns his tears into mud.

    "It's gonna be ok," I say, "kita boleh, kita boleh."

    He nods silently at this, and we start taking steps forward.

    We move slowly through the jungle. Jia gong's not a heavy man, but all that alcohol's made him sloppy and uncoordinated, and it doesn't take long for us to tire out. With my arm wrapped around his torso and his arm held to my back, our body heat mixes with all that humidity, and I can feel him sweating into my clothes, and I'm doing the same, and the smell of all this sweat and still air exhausts us even more, and we're forced to take breaks, leaning on trees for a few minutes before continuing again.

    Jia gong's acting off now, is being really quiet. He keeps looking back at the way we came, and he looks scared. I can't get that image of that falling body out of my head, and I figure he must be thinking about the same thing.

    The sunlight that bores past the canopy shifts from its light yellow into a darker orange as the sun begins to set, and it makes me wish we could move faster. My stomach growls, and I realise how hungry I'm getting.

    I hold tight onto jia gong as we step over a large tree root nestled with granite rocks that make balance hard. I try to help lift jia gong's foot over them, but the bottom part of his foot grazes against the top bit of a rock, and I hear him gasp, and he winces hard, grabs onto my shirt, and balls it up tight in his fist until the pain starts to disappear.

"Sorry," I say.

Jia gong doesn't say anything, but he plants a wet kiss behind my ear and pats me twice with his palm.

Evening comes and covers everything in warm orange sunlight that causes shadows to grow from dense greenery, starting to obscure what we can see in the jungle.

More mosquitos begin to appear, and I find myself scratching thoughtlessly at bug bites all over my arms and legs, the skin broken in some areas and sticky with thick sweat. Salty sweat mixes with small open wounds, and I feel stinging all across my legs.

I look over to jia gong and I can tell he's really drunk now. His eyes roll around, and while he's let his injured foot go limp, his good foot's now a wobbly, unbalanced mess, and we nearly fall over a couple of times if not for the trees all around us to lean on for support, though I look down at my arms and see that rough bark has left tiny cuts and scrapes across the skin.

I'm sweating hard and hungry, and I can hear the sound of a flowing stream close by. "We're...we're nearly there, right?"

"Good boy, ah, good boy," jia gong says, patting me on the side with the hand he's holding onto me with.

We take a couple more steps to what I'm sure is our camp when that smell of rot returns in the periphery. It doesn't take long before the smell starts to intensify and the air is covered in thick, fermented bitterness.

We take a few more steps forward and finally see the clearing in the distance and our unmistakable navy blue tent.

I could cry from relief even though this smell of rot is fully overpowering at this point, making me feel nauseous and feverish.

"We're here!" I yell, squeezing jia gong's shoulder.

I am helping jia gong hobble up to the edge of the clearing when I see a shape on the ground, opposite our tent and close to some ferns. Jia gong's eyes trail down to the shape, and the moment he sees it properly, he starts screaming and lets go of me and falls to the ground, and I see his eyes are massive, and he's screaming over and over again and starts to desperately crawl away from our campsite in full panic.

I look down at what jia gong saw and see that it is a woman's bare body resting on her side, positioned so she's looking right at the entrance of our tent. Her body is perfectly still, and from where I'm standing, I can only see her back and her long black hair. There is a bullet's nasty exit wound coming out her back, below her shoulder blade, and there is broken-up red flesh and yellow fat pushed upward and outwards to form a jagged, flowering wound.

Panic and dread mix with adrenaline, and the humid smell of rot is so intense it is almost solid in the air, feels like I am inhaling rancid fat into my lungs, and I turn away from the body and double over, trying to vomit into the ground, racking my chest with big heaving, though nothing but thick saliva and bile comes up as I've barely eaten anything.

Nauseous and unsteady, I look up to see jia gong has crawled up to the base of a massive tree and has propped his back up against it. I walk towards him and feel another wave of nausea forcing me to my knees and making me heave at the ground, with nothing but stringy saliva coming down, and I'm exhausted from the effort, and I get back up on my feet and stumble up to jia gong.

I look at this tree jia gong is sitting under and realise I cannot see its top past the thick leafy canopy. Evening is in full force now, and saturated, dim orange sunlight shines through and casts everything in its amber glow, while everything the sunlight can't reach is obscured in dark green dusk.

Jia gong's eyes are large, and even though he's swaying from alcohol, I can still see all that fear plainly on his face, and it makes me feel horrible.

My throat is extremely dry, and I'd do anything for some water.

"Cannot go, cannot go." Jia gong says, shaking his head and looking at our campsite. From here, I can still see our navy blue tent, and my eyes can't help but gravitate towards the sight of the top of the body's head of black hair, though greenery covers the rest of her body from where we're sitting. Looking at her hair makes me feel dizzy, and I have to fight the urge to vomit, so I look away.

"I think…I think we can just leave. Just leave and reach the car and go home," I say, but then I look down at jia gong's foot and see that the skin has turned an agitated red colour with a few purple splotches blooming around the top part of his foot, and it is about twice the size of his good foot.

Jia gong didn't hear or didn't understand what I said, and he's staring at his foot too, and he gingerly adjusts it and winces when he moves it too suddenly.

"What do we do?" I ask, trying to ignore the intense feeling of dread building up in my stomach and the thirst in my throat so dry it hurts to swallow.

"Good boy, good boy," jia gong nods, motioning me to come towards him with his palms.

I crouch down and inch closer to jia gong, and when I'm close enough, he pulls me into a big hug. He wraps his arms around me and brings my head towards him with his palm, and he kisses me on the head over and over again, and I can smell the vodka when he breathes and I hear him sobbing and realise he's crying, and he's kissing me over and over and over again and stroking my hair and holding me close to him, and I can't help it, and I start crying too, big ugly sobs that rack my whole body, and I wrap my arms around him and hug him back, and I can feel all that sweat drenched in the back of his shirt, and I hold him as tight as I can, and I tell him I love him so much.

"Good boy, yah, good boy," he says again, patting my back, kissing my forehead, and letting me free of his hug.

I sit back, and I can see his eyes are all puffy with tears, and he's got a river of snot coming down that he's wiping away with the back of his hands, and I say, still sobbing, "It's okay…it's okay. One night," I say, pointing at his foot, "one night, and then tomorrow we go."

I feel something light stinging on my neck, and I slap at the itch and see that it was a fat, blood-engorged mosquito, now flattened and staining the grooves of my palm a bright red colour.

I swallow and feel how dry my throat is, and I look at our camp clearing, knowing the stream is right past it.

What feels like an hour passes, and dusk is coming in full force, and we don't even have a fire, and my body is full of itchy mosquito bites, and the sound of all those cicadas has gotten even louder, constant white noise as jia gong and I sit under this tree and wait for the time to pass. I can feel the bits of dry dirt in my socks that have mixed with sweat to turn into sticky mud, and I untie my damp shoes and pull my socks off to see pale, wrinkly toes.

I pull my phone out of my pocket and see that the battery has dropped to 51% now. The time is 7:51 p.m., and I am only getting thirstier with every minute, and I can't stop thinking about water and how badly I need it.

I try to swallow what's in my mouth, but it's completely dry, and it makes my throat sting.

I look to jia gong, at his inflamed ankle, and I say, "I need water."

He looks up at me, starting to sober up now but still really out of it, and he raises a pained eyebrow and says, "Har?"

I sigh and press my tongue against the roof of my mouth, feel the dryness, and I say, "我要水."

He nods, and he reaches down to his pocket and offers me the last quarter of vodka in his plastic bottle.

I laugh a little and look at that vodka at the bottom, clear, just like water.

I figure that…maybe it can only help, and so I take the bottle, uncap it, put it up to my lips, tilt it up, taste burning bitter fermentation, and I wince, bring the bottle down, smack my lips, and feel nothing but more dryness, and now this pungent, flowery bitterness mixes with the smell of rot I'd only just been getting used to, and I can't help but dry heave.

I stand up and look at the clearing, the top of the body's head of hair, and have to look away from that immediate, heavy dizziness.

I pass the bottle back to jia gong, and I say, "我要水."

His eyes go wide at this. "不可以."

I look up at the clearing and figure I can probably walk around our campsite to the stream.

"I don't even need to go close to the body," I say.

"不可以," he shakes his head again.

"I'm so thirsty," I say.

"No." Jia gong grabs the tips of my fingers.

"我会来," I say.

"No, no, no! No! No! No! No! No! No! No!" Jia gong yells, over and over again.

"I'm sorry," I say, feeling my throat closing in on itself with thirst, and I start walking towards the stream.

"No! No! No!" Jia gong keeps yelling, and then I think I hear him crying, but I'm pushing past thick, heavy leaves and feeling the cool, damp earth on my bare feet, and I figure he's just being crazy now. The water's right there, and we don't even really know what's happening.

That smell of rot is so intense now, and I can feel it like a solid rotten tooth in the back of my throat.

I step past purple sea-urchin-like flowers out into the stream and feel the cold current between my toes. I see the big, rotting buffalo a couple of metres upstream from where I am, more of a general, large shape now in the dark orange evening, and I figure it's good that at least I get to drink from clean freshwater so long as I give the buffalo enough space, and I bend down, scoop clear river water up in my palms and take a big drink, and immediately taste slimy fermented rot, and I swallow the water anyway from how thirsty I am, but I look up in confusion and see that I hadn't actually walked far away from the buffalo body to take a drink of water, but I'd walked right up beside it instead.

I start to feel like something is really wrong, and it makes me start to panic, and my head feels heavy. I look at the dead water buffalo body, its head looking away from me and upstream, and I see now that there are Chinese characters etched perfectly in the skin close to its backbone, and I hadn't noticed it before from how dark red the wound is in contrast to the buffalo's black skin, and the characters read, 溪流中总有一具尸体, and I have no idea what it means.

    Thirst is still thick in my throat, and so I wade over to the left of the buffalo and try to drink from this cleaner water again, and the water still tastes bitter, and I look up and see that I haven't moved.

    I cup more water and bend down so that I'm basically drinking right from the flowing stream, and I immediately start to feel so much better as my body's calling for it disappears.

    I stand up again and start walking back upstream of the water buffalo's body, and I see our campsite and the backpacks we left behind, and I start thinking about all those snacks, and I feel how hungry I am, and even though the smell in the air is constant, I can't stop thinking about how badly I want a salty cracker on my tongue.

    I walk past where I must have come out into the stream and figure I'm getting used to this smell anyway, so I might as well grab a bunch of those salty crackers and run right back to jia gong. Maybe even grab some alcohol for him, I mean, why not, right, he's already fucked his leg up, alcohol can only help at this point, and so I keep walking until I'm at the edge of our camp clearing, and I can see the body fully now.

    A pale, dark purple naked woman, sagging slightly with decomposition, and the stench pierces my nostrils and makes my eyes water. There's a bullet wound in her chest.

    Looking at her makes me so dizzy I nearly fall over backwards, but I manage to step back in time, and I look away as fast as I can, and I figure if I'm doing this, I'm just gonna grab the backpack with the food and run. Fuck the alcohol.

I sprint up beside our tent, grab the backpack by one of its straps, and sprint towards where jia gong is.

As I'm running, I feel a sudden intense weight over my whole body, and that dizziness comes over me, bringing me to a complete stop, and this weight over my whole body only gets heavier and heavier until I'm forced down to my knees with all that weight, the air around me a gravity pushing me downwards, and the dizziness in my head so strong I have to stop myself from puking up water, and I look around, feeling confused, and see that I am right between our tent and the woman's dead body, and this heightened gravity forces me all the way down until my face is on the ground, and I start to feel so tired. Deep exhaustion coming in with the immense weight of all this air. I can feel the gravity bringing my eyelids down and even with all this fear and adrenaline going through me, I try to fight this tiredness and keep my eyes open, but my eyes feel slippery, and I can't seem to focus on anything anymore, and I can't help but fall asleep.

Dreamless sleep and I wake up in pitch black night to a piercing ringing sound in my ears, tinnitus amplified to massive levels, a wall of sound surrounding me and pushing me downwards, immense gravity with this ringing in my ears, and I try to move my body but I can't under all this weight.

I'm breathing heavy now, full of panic, and I can feel a scream building in my throat, but I can't get it out.

Rancid stench of rot in the air, competing with this ringing sound in my ears, so overwhelming I need to get up and leave the smell, but still, my body is totally paralysed by this weight, and I can't see a thing in all this dark.

I try to shift my body, and I can feel coarse nylon against my skin.

In all this dark, I realise I can feel arms around my body, and something is making contact with my back, and I can feel something touching me, something against the back of my head, something pressing into my back, all the way down to my tailbone.

Panic in my whole body like when blood rushes back to a limb that's fallen asleep, and again I try to squirm against this immense weight and ringing in my ears, so loud it feels like my whole body is vibrating from the frequency.

I try to shift again, and I feel these arms wrapped around me, and I feel that they are cold and wet with loose, bloated skin, and with that stench of decay all over me, I realise it is the body holding me from behind, and I'm trying to scream so hard, and I'm trying to move, but this ringing in my ears keeps pushing down into the ground.

I have no idea how much time has passed, and I am here, in the dark, hyperventilating, trying to squirm my way free when I feel that my toes are moving. When I try hard enough, I can bend the tips of my fingers.

I focus on this now and try to block out that constant, high-pitched drone.

I focus on my toes, move them up and down. Up, and down, and then my fingers, and I curl them and spread them open over and over again.

I keep doing this until I can feel an ankle shift, and I keep thinking about my body and push out every other thought, and try to ignore this pungent, fermented stench, and soon both ankles are moving up and down, and then I focus on my wrists, and soon I'm able to wiggle my arms, too.

I start to be able to hear my breathing past the high-pitched ringing, and I can start moving my knees, and then I move my legs higher up, and then I'm able to move my torso, and I start to squirm away from the body pressed tight against me.

It takes so much effort, pushing myself against this thick gravity, but as soon as I start to move so that the body isn't making contact with my back anymore, I can feel more of my limbs moving, and this weight is starting to lift, and then all at once I find my whole body moving, and the ringing disappears, and my vocal cords are free, and I'm screaming until my throat's raw, and still groggy from all that weight, I stumble back up to my feet in the pitch-black dark, and I just run forward and straight into more nylon, and I try to push against the nylon, and it doesn't budge, and I walk around more and feel the walls of where I am and realise I am in our tent, and I keep pressing my palms up against the tent fabric until I push hard enough against what must be the entrance, and I push with too much force, and I hear a zipper give, and I fall through the tent opening and out into the humid, pitch-black jungle.

"JIA GONG!" I scream into the night, no idea what time it is or where I am.

"JIA GONG!" I scream again, and hear nothing but the chirping sounds of insects and hoots from some animal.

"JIA GONG!" I scream again, standing up and feeling the cool ground against my bare feet. I feel a weight in my pocket and remember it's my phone. I pull it out, and I tap the screen on and see that it is 3:30 a.m., and I only have 23% battery left.

I tap the flashlight on, and pale white light illuminates everything in a feverish fluorescent glow that causes the things lit up to cast long shadows out in every direction.

I start running to where I must've left jia gong and keep yelling his name. "JIA GONG! JIA GONG! I'M HERE! 我在这里!!"

I reach what feels like a familiar spot in the jungle, but I don't know anymore. I walk up to a large tree that must have been where we were resting. He shouldn't have even been able to move with that ankle.

I bring both my palms up to my mouth and yell, "JIAAAAA GOOOOOONG!!!" But the words just get swallowed up by the jungle's constant white noise, and I don't hear jia gong's voice calling back.

I can't stop myself from breathing fast, and I can feel panic building up in my feet, and if jia gong's not here, then for sure he's back at the car already. It's so late, he probably hobbled his way there and is waiting for me. It makes sense.

I feel the sensation of something looking at me, a pressure boring into the back of my head, and it pushes my legs into a sprint to get as far away from this spot as possible, and I run to the sound of flowing water.

I push past sharp leaves that dig into my skin and feel thorns rub against and puncture raw insect bites on my thighs and feet, and I keep running with my flashlight up, illuminating everything a couple of metres in front of me in a cone of white light that is quickly swallowed up by the jungle night.

The sound of running water grows, and I smell the thick, fragrant, sweet sappy scent of pandan, and I point my flashlight forward and see that it is a small field of pandan, their long leaves spiky at the ends and sharp on the sides. They smell like freshly cut grass mixed with melted sugar.

I step through the pandan, feel their tips poke at my thighs, and I break past their leaves and step into the fresh cold stream.

I point my flashlight up and see the buffalo body upstream, and with that, I turn around and walk downstream, trying to retrace our steps.

My feet slip on algae-covered rocks, and I fall into the stream and hit my cheek against a sharp rock, and I feel the pain radiating through my whole head, and cold water soaking into my clothes and water burning up my nose, and I get up as quickly as I can and spit and feel my throbbing cheek and ignore the pain and how cold the water is.

My phone was dipped in the water, and a warning shows up on the screen now: *do not recharge until water has dried from charging port.*

The flashlight still works, and I look at the top and see I only have 15% battery left, and I pick up the pace and try to wade through the water faster.

My foot slips on another slimy wet rock, but I manage to catch myself with my hands, but in doing so, I slam my phone face down against a dry, hard rock, and though the flashlight is still on, the whole screen turns into a cracked blobby mess of pink, blue, and green LCD liquid.

"Fuck!" I breathe, and I keep going forward.

I shine the flashlight up and look on either side of the stream. Where had we come out from last time?

I wade a little further downstream, raise the flashlight up again, and see something familiar: a small disturbance in the vegetation where some bushes have been flattened, and maybe it was where we'd walked out from.

I don't have much battery left, and I can't stay here all night, so I decide to follow this path, and I step out of the stream and back onto damp, cool earth.

I'm panting from the exhaustion of wading through water and trying to keep my balance. The smell of rot in the air is completely absent now, and it is just the thick smell of wet earth and humidity.

I see a trail in the dirt and I start to follow it.

I follow the trail until I reach another patch where the greenery has been flattened by someone stepping over it, and I follow these clues until I reach a familiar-looking tree, and I shine my flashlight to its base and see those Chinese characters jia gong had used for navigating us into the jungle: 一直有一只观鸟.

I sigh with relief, knowing the car is just ahead, and jia gong has to be, too, and so I start yelling, "JIA GONG! JIA GONG!! 你在哪里?!"

I don't hear anything in response, and it fills me with a heavy feeling of dread.

I shine my phone flashlight on the dirt trail and follow it until I see a big shape in the dark ahead, and I bring the light up and see that it is jia gong's car, collecting dried-out leaves on its windshield.

"Jia gong?!" I call out again, and hear nothing but the constant drone of cicadas.

I walk up to the car door, try to pull it open, and realise it's locked, and jia gong had the keys.

"Fuck…" I breathe, and all I want to do is sit down and cry.

I walk around the car and try all the doors, and all of them are locked tight, I mean…of course.

I shine my phone light down on the dirt trail the car drove through to get here, and I follow this trail now.

My flashlight finally dies, and I'm covered in deep night, but I take a breath, try to stay calm, and I make sure my bare feet stick to the dry, dusty trail.

I walk for what feels like many minutes in the dark until I start to hear the sounds of cars driving down the highway.

The trail grows wider and dry dirt gives way to sharp, loose gravel, and I walk until I see the dull orange glow of streetlights in the distance, and I keep walking until I step out of thick jungle and onto the side of an empty highway.

There is nothing here now but the sound of wind and the occasional car in the distance. Headlights show up ahead, and a car drives right past me way too fast to even notice I'm here, and I'm too late to yell for help.

I realise I'm still holding my phone in my hand, and so I put it in my pocket and lift my thumb up to hitchhike.

I can see dark purple sunrise appearing on the horizon, coming up behind more dense rainforest on the other side of the road. In the dark, all I can see is the jungle's massive outline: the fluffy edges of trees and the silhouette of occasional treetops growing above the canopy. Some animal makes a long, drawn-out hoot, and I hope someone picks me up off the side of the road soon.

Acknowledgements

ALRIGHT. So you finished the book. (Well, unless you skipped all the way to the end like a crazy person who should consider some extreme form of therapy.) Thanks so much for reading it! It means a whole lot to me, and I hope you enjoyed reading these stories :)

I'm self-publishing this book, which means I get to do whatever tf I want, and I can be as unprofessional as I want to be in my acknowledgements. OH, LOOK, MEL, MR. EDITOR, iS, ThIs, a, COmmA, sPl,IcE? What even is a comma splice anyway?? OH AND LOOK… …. … … ,,, .. ,,.. ,…,. ,…, .,. ,.,.,.,.….,,,.,,,,…, .. ,.,. Ha ha

In all seriousness, though, thank you so much to the editor of this collection, Melchior Dudley. He has edited everything literally for free, which is so incredibly generous, and his edits have really brought the whole book to a level of polish that I could never accomplish on my own, especially since my grammar is god-awful.

Thank you so much to Nim Holden for her fantastic work in creating the cover lettering, also for the extremely generous sum of completely free, and thank you so much to Voja World, who can be found on Instagram at Voja_World. I licensed the front and back cover from him, and godddaaaaaaamn is it a good look.

Thank you so much to Emily Folan for consistently being one of the first readers of all my stories and for understanding story and space and giving feedback that is incredibly helpful. Seriously, so many of these stories would be so much worse without your help. Thank you so much.

Thank you to Liam St. John for his help in suggesting a pretty major edit in the story, *Diphenhydramine, for Allergies and Other Things*. The story was much worse until I cut a massive chunk out as suggested by him, and thank you for being a part of my writing community in Peterborough and a good friend.

Thank you so much to Dorothy Cheng for correcting historical inaccuracies and just generally giving suggestions that made the setting of Malaysia in *Deep Green Gravity* that much more concrete and present. She is basically my sister. Love you so much, Dot!!!

Thank you to Rachel Litchman for making various suggestions in a number of different short stories that helped to generally make these pieces easier to read and feel truer to their spaces. So glad to know you Rachel!

Thank you to all the various professors and teachers in my life who have helped me gain a better understanding of just what I am trying to do, but then also showing me what other artists, in general, have done, along with showing me how little I know about anything. The knowledge has been invaluable, and this book wouldn't have been possible without the privilege of this knowledge and education, so thank you to: Rob Winger, Kelly Egan, Charmaine Eddy, Dave Griffith, Mika Perrine, Francine Harris, Lewis MacLeod, Stephen Brown, Katherine Chittick, Brent Bellamy, Nadine Changfoot, Martin Arnold, Janette Platana, and Emily

Bruusgard. Seriously, learning about storytelling and art as a whole through education is something that has impacted my life in so many ways I cannot count them.

Thank you again, so much, to my mom, Christine Chee, who is just simply an amazing and strong woman. Thank you so much for everything and for supporting me so much and for helping me get this far. All this would be literally completely impossible not only without you but also without your constant support. Thank you.

Thank you to the land that these stories come from. The places I live in automatically have a massive impact on the stories that are made, and so thank you to Peterborough, stolen land that is known originally as Nogojiwanong. You can be a rough and difficult place to live in sometimes, but you are also so full of beauty. Thank you to Malaysia, my home country. Its food, smells, humidity, pollution, people, and rainforests will never leave my bones.

Finally, thank you to the people who are a part of my life. Stories cannot be made without community, and community informs story and space, and then space and story inform community. The friends and the important people in my life constantly become a mix of characters, and the words I hear turn into the ways people speak in stories.

I consider these people to be such an important part of my life. Thank you so much to: Rodney Simon, Emma Johns, Ken Looi, Shun-Li, Zachary Barmania, Sass Mueller, Jamie John, Edward Manuel, Elesh Vengadesan-Lee, Jordana Valerie Allen-Shim, Aurko Sen, Mann Woei Wong, Chance McGuigan, Aurynn JP, Sendra

Uebele, Beth Morrow, Oasis Vali, Victoria Cheng, Sophie Henslee, James Holton, Cam Lasuarez, Riku Inoue, Graham Wylie, Tyler Majer, Adam Tario, Alden Hunter, and Mody Ari. There are absolutely people I have missed in this list. But thank you to everyone who is a part of my community. It means so much.

Thank you to the animals in my life. Nature is constant, and we constantly interact with nature whether we recognize it or not. Thank you to: Chernobyl, Pekoe, Earl Grey, Scooby, Little Grey, and Morey. Thank you to Canadian and Malaysian places such as Algonquin, the large lakes of Midwest–eastern North America, FRIM, Bako National Park, and Broga Hill.

I am including all these places and people in my acknowledgements because at the end of the day, we're all in this messy, pretty, and strange shitshow together. Art doesn't exist in a vacuum. It comes from community and it comes from the places we go to, and the stories we tell each other. It comes from a whole lot of love and solidarity even in the toughest of times.

Thank you so much, yet again, for reading this book. It means a lot.

Feel free to reach out at: shaunleephuah@gmail.com

or follow me on the horrible social media sites that are Instagram or Twitter @mnolololo for updates on future works, or if you are interested in the video art projects I also do.

FUCK SHIT PISS SHIT PISS SHIT FUCK.

Anyway BYEEEE.

```
_____$$$$$$__
_____$$$$(a)$$::7
_____$$$$$$$$:/
____$$$$$$$$,
__§??`?? ?`???$$,
§??`??`????$$$$$$,
§???????$$$$$$$$$$s
$?`??`???$$$$$$$$$ $$$,
§?????????$$$$$$$$$$$$$s,,,,
_`j§???`????`?$$$$$$$$$$$$$$$s,,
____"§??? ??????$$$$$$____$$$$$$s,,
_____"r§?????__$$$$_____$$$$$$
_____//___//_ _____$$
_____//-__//
```

Manufactured by Amazon.ca
Bolton, ON